I0631260

William M. (William Mackergo) Taylor

The Lost Found and the Wanderer Welcomed

William M. (William Mackergo) Taylor

The Lost Found and the Wanderer Welcomed

ISBN/EAN: 9783744792615

Printed in Europe, USA, Canada, Australia, Japan

Cover: Foto ©Andreas Hilbeck / pixelio.de

More available books at **www.hansebooks.com**

The Lost Found,

AND

THE WANDERER WELCOMED.

BY

WILLIAM M. TAYLOR, D.D.,

MINISTER OF THE BROADWAY TABERNACLE, NEW YORK.

———

NEW YORK:

SCRIBNER, ARMSTRONG AND COMPANY,

1873.

Entered according to act of Congress, in the year 1872, by
SCRIBNER, ARMSTRONG & COMPANY,
In the office of the Librarian of Congress at Washington.

CONTENTS.

PAGE

THE LOST SHEEP. 3

THE LOST COIN 33

THE PRODIGAL SON.

    I.—THE DEPARTURE 59

    II.—THE RESOLUTION........................... 85

    III.—THE RETURN............... 115

    IV.—THE ELDER BROTHER 147

THE LOST SHEEP.

"Then drew near unto him all the publicans and sinners for to hear him.

"And the Pharisees and scribes murmured, saying, This man receiveth sinners, and eateth with them.

"And he spake this parable unto them, saying,

"What man of you, having an hundred sheep, if he lose one of them, doth not leave the ninety and nine in the wilderness, and go after that which is lost, until he find it?

"And when he hath found it, he layeth it on his shoulders, rejoicing.

"And when he cometh home, he calleth together his friends and neighbors, saying unto them, Rejoice with me ; for I have found my sheep which was lost.

"I say unto you, that likewise joy shall be in heaven over one sinner that repenteth, more than over ninety and nine just persons, which need no repentance."

LUKE, xv., 1-7.

THE LOST SHEEP.

THE personal ministry of Christ had a marvellous attractiveness for the degraded outcasts of the Jewish population, and, wherever He went, the Pariahs of the people gathered round Him, in listening multitudes. Everywhere " the common people heard Him gladly," and among the crowds that thronged around Him, the hated tax-gatherers, whose extortions made them obnoxious to their fellow-citizens; the openly immoral, whose vices were abhorred by their more respectable neighbors; and those poor waifs of womanhood, the fallen ones who trafficked in their own dishonor, were specially conspicuous. Nor is it difficult to account for this; for though He loathed the sins, He loved the sinners, and stretched out to them the hand of sympathy and succor. He did not draw

them to Himself by making them think less of
the guilt which they had incurred, but by awakening in them a sense of the loss which they
had sustained, and by implanting in them the
hope of restoration. . His purity alone might
have repelled them, even as it drove the demons
shrieking from His presence; His love alone
might have done no more than soothe them by
the manifestation of his interest in them; but
the gospel which He proclaimed to them, and
which announced that even the vilest might be
received into the favor of the Lord, won their
interest, and drew them to His side. Others
had denounced their iniquity, but that only made
them tremble, as their fathers did at the base of
Sinai. He took them by the hand, and, by His
declaration of the possibility of their receiving
forgiveness, and of their recovering that image of
God which they had lost, He revived the better
nature which had been dead within them, and
dissipated that despair which had made them re-
gardless alike of God and man. This was the
magnetism that attracted them; and as they
hung upon His hope-inspiring words, they said,
"Never man spake like this man."

There was much, too, in His mode of treating

them that disposed them to flock around Him. The solemn purists of the land held them at a distance. They passed them by, like the priest and Levite in the parable, "on the other side." They acted as if they would be polluted by the most cursory intercourse with them. They seemed to think that all their duty toward them was discharged, if they simply held aloof from them. But here was One whose character was unsullied, and whose life was blameless, who yet did not think it beneath Him to put Himself, for the time, on a level with them, by receiving them into His company, and sitting down with them at table ; and such was the effect of His fellowship upon them, that they were elevated and ennobled by its influence, and left His presence more drawn to holiness and heaven than they had ever felt before. Others had driven them downwards, but Jesus had lifted them up. He made them feel their importance as immortal beings. He opened up to them the way to happiness and to God, and helped them to enter upon it. He taught them to respect themselves by showing them that they were the objects of the Divine compassion, and by telling them that He had come to seek and save them ; and so it was that, while the spiritually and intellectually proud stood haughtily aside from Him, the publicans and sinners pressed near to hear His sayings.

But this very success among the despised of the people still further alienated the self-righteous from Him. Already, indeed, they had been repelled by His searching discourses, which insisted so constantly on inward holiness, as distinguished from mere outward morality or ritualistic observances ; but when they saw the character of those who were thus clustering round him, they sneeringly said, " *This man receiveth sinners, and eateth with them.*" Usually, the sting of a taunt lies in its truth ; but, in this instance, what they meant in contemptuous scorn was in reality the highest glory of the Lord, and is to-day the sum and substance of the gospel which we preach, When John the Baptist sent from his prison to assure himself of the genuineness of the Messiahship of Jesus, the Lord replied by working many miracles before the eyes of his messengers, and by telling them to go their way and show their master what they had seen ; adding, as the most important evidence of the divinity of His mission, and the greatest miracle of all—" And to

the poor the gospel is preached." Nor was he
mistaken in this ; for grander, more glorious, and,
as an evidence of Christianity, more convincing
by far, than any miracle on the bodies of men,
was the moral miracle which, by the power of His
Spirit, was wrought on the vilest of those who believed in His words, and which we may see daily
repeated before our eyes. " This man receiveth
sinners." We thank thee, Scribe, for teaching us
the words ; let them be caught up and repeated by
echoing voices in every city and in every land,
until every child of Adam has experienced their
truth. *Sinners*—not righteous men, not rich, not
noble, not mighty, not moral, but sinners—no
matter how vile and guilty they may have been—
here are His words :—" Him that cometh unto
me I will in no wise cast out." *Receiveth* sinners
—not coldly treateth them, not holdeth them
aloof, not regardeth them with freezing dignity
and stately solemnity, but receiveth them to His
heart, and spreadeth for them a table, at which
He counts them His most valued guests. It was
meant as a sneer ; and yet, all unconsciously,
these Scribes and Pharisees, in giving it expression, did preach the gospel more simply and more
truly than it has often been proclaimed by sur-

pliced bishop or by trained minister. What can we say more, or better, in telling the good news than this—" Jesus receiveth sinners?" Guilty one! this morning, He will receive thee ; for are not these his words, " Come unto me, and I will give you rest?'

This was not the only occasion on which such a taunt was uttered. Frequently the same thing was thrown in the Saviour's teeth, and he had two ways of meeting it. Sometimes he repelled it; by trying to awaken those who used it to a sense of their own sinfulness. Thus, when, at the call of Matthew, He sat down to the banquet which the publican had prepared, and the Phar- isees said to his disciples, " Why eateth your mas- ter with publicans and sinners?" He made an- swer, " They that are whole need not a physi- cian, but they that are sick ;" and then sought to reveal their own sickness to them by saying, " Go ye and learn what that meaneth, I will have mer- cy, and not sacrifice." That is to say, He re- minded them of the inner and spiritual nature of all acceptable service, that He might the better convince them of the utter formalism of their re- ligious exercises. Sometimes, again, He justified His conduct by dwelling on the mercy of God to

sinners, and setting forth the great object of His
mission to mankind. This was the course He
followed at Jericho, when to those who gibed
Him for going to the house of Zacchæus, He
said, " The Son of Man is come to seek and to
save that which was lost." As if He had replied,
" I have come to seek the lost ; even, therefore,
if Zacchæus should be as bad as you represent
him to be, I am only fulfilling the real purpose of
my ministry when I seek to save him. The man
who is most seriously wounded ought to have the
surgeon's *first* attention ; so those whom sin has
most defaced should have the Saviour's earliest
care."

Now, this latter argument is that which Jesus
employs in the present instance ; for in the parables which follow He illustrates the great redemption work by a series of pictures, each of
which leads up to, and centres in, the happiness
of the Godhead in receiving sinners ; and He
would have His hearers thence infer, that in working among the despised among men, He was truly
representing the Divine Father, whose eternal
Son he was ; while, in ridiculing His efforts,
they were altogether out of sympathy with those
heavenly intelligences among whom there is joy

over one sinner that repenteth. Behold how out of evil God ever bringeth good! We owe the parable of the prodigal son to the gibes of of the Pharisees. They say that the sandal-wood gives forth its richest fragrance to the axe that cuts it; and certainly no diviner words ever issued from the Redeemer's lips than these, which came in answer to a sneer. The cross is God's reply to men's insulting iniquity, and the story of the prodigal is Christ's only response to the scorn of His assailants.

In seeking to expound these parables, as in this and a few other discourses I mean to do, it is needful to mark, in the outset, not only the one great purpose for which they were all related, but also the different phases of the one subject which they individually present. This will, of course, come out more prominently as we enter more fully on the explanation of each. Meanwhile, it may be enough to indicate the points of agreement and diversity between them. They all agree in representing the lost sinner as the object of God's solicitude, and the repentant sinner as the occasion of celestial joy. But they differ in the views which they give of the process of the sinner's restoration and recovery.

The first two parables show us the Divine agency in the sinner's recovery; the last lets us see the result of that agency in the sinner's own activity. The first two set before us God seeking the sinner, together with the Divine joy when the sinner is found; the last gives special prominence to the sinner's own voluntary return to God. The first two have their starting-point in the heart of God, and we see in them the Heavenly Father yearning over his lost child, and taking means to find him and bring him back. The last has its starting-point in the sinner himself, and shows us his wandering and his return, as well as his reception. But there is no discrepancy here. Rather the full truth is to be attained by the combination of them all; and when you see the prodigal coming to himself, and hear him saying, "I will arise and go to my Father," you are to understand that already the Good Shepherd has been there to seek him, and the Holy Spirit has been striving within him. Such is the grandeur of the work of redemption, that no one parable can adequately portray it; and therefore here, we have three given to us, that in the union of them all, we might have a more complete understanding of the wondrous theme.

But this is not all. Each parable brings before us a particular kind of sinful experience. The first, in the wandering sheep, portrays the helpless sinner ; the second, in the lost coin, depicts the man who has fallen so low as to have lost the stamp of his Creator, and the consciousness of his degradation ; and the third, in the rebellious son, sets before us the sinner who is knowing and deliberate in his iniquity. Corresponding to this difference in the description of the sinner is that which we find in the delineation of his recovery ; for in the first parable we have the work of the divine Son, the great Good Shepherd ; in the second, that of the Holy Spirit ; and in the third, the Eternal Father's eager desire for the salvation of sinners, and His great delight in their deliverance. In none of the three is there any direct reference to that cross whereon Jesus gave Himself a sacrifice for human guilt ; but we may not forget, that He who uttered them was, at the very moment, straitened for the accomplishment of that baptism of blood wherewith for us he was baptized, and we must read them all under the shadow of Calvary.

But now, leaving these general topics, let us look a little at the teaching of the parable

of the lost sheep. It was spoken by Jesus on another occasion, as we find recorded in the 18th
chapter of Matthew's Gospel, at the 12th verse.
But there it was designed to illustrate the importance of even one soul in the Heavenly Father's
eye. Here it was intended to teach especially
these four things : *first*, God's yearning over the
sinner ; *second*, The helplessness of the sinner to
return to God ; *third*, The means used by God for
the sinner's recovery ; and *fourth*, The joy manifested by God over the sinner's return. Let us
take up these in the order now advanced.

I. There is, first, *God's yearning over the sinner*.
Usually, in depicting a lost sinner, we dwell on
the miseries which he has brought upon himself.
But this and the succeeding parables differ from
the ordinary representations of the subject, in
that they set before us the loss which God has
sustained in the wandering and rebellion of His
children. Here it is symbolized by the losing of
one out of a hundred sheep ; in the next parable,
by the losing of one out of ten coins ; and in the
third, by the losing of one out of two sons. Now,
I know that it would be perilous to press a mere
human analogy too far, when we are speaking

about God. I admit also that, strictly and absolutely, God cannot be said to lose anything, and
that He dwelleth evermore in happiness, which
nothing can either destroy or becloud. But still
the figure of these parables has, somewhere and
somehow, a real significance. We cannot, we
must not, eliminate from this losing of the sheep,
of the money, of the son, all reference to the effect of the sinner's rebellion upon God. They
mean that Jehovah has missed something which
He had possessed. They mean that from His
point of view the sinner is as something lost is,
to its former owner. At first there was a human
voice in the choral harmony of creation's an-
them, which rose so sweetly on the ear of God;
but when sin made its appearance, that voice
dropped out, and He marked its absence with
as much regret as Deity can feel. Nay, there
was a special reason why God should miss human allegiance, for man alone, of all His creatures, so far as we know at least, was created
in God's image. In him alone could Jehovah
see the perfect, though miniature, representation
of Himself; but when he sinned, that image
was defaced, and God lost the complacency
which He had in him before. Or, to put it

more simply, when man fell, God lost the honor
and service which ought to have been rendered
by him ; the affection with which He ought to
have been regarded by him ; and the glory
which would have resulted to Him had he answered the great design for which he was created. Nor let it be supposed that, in putting
this prominently forward, I am insisting on what
is of no importance ; for, in the consciousness
of this loss on the part of God, I find the root
from which at length grew up the great work of
redemption. And, depraved though we ourselves
may be, we yet possess so much of our prime-
val resemblance to God as to be able thoroughly to understand this. We do not like to lose
anything. No matter how trivial or unimportant
the object may be, we will search, and search,
and search again, rather than give it up as irrecoverable ; and the more we value that which
we have lost, the more earnest will be our exertions to find it. If it be an animal, or a sum of
money, we will go hither and thither ourselves,
and engage our neighbors in the quest, if by
any means we may be successful ; and if it be a
son, all the great depths of our hearts will be
stirred within us, as we set out and track him in

his wanderings, nor will we give over our efforts until we come, either on himself, or on his grave. Now, there must be something akin to all this in that God, whose image was at first enstamped upon us. I say not, indeed, that the loss of His human children caused Him positive unhappiness; and yet, after all, why need I be so chary? Do not the Holy Scriptures speak of Him as being grieved? Do they not represent Him as soliloquizing within Himself thus: "How shall I give thee up, Ephraim? How shall I deliver thee, Israel? How shall I make thee as Admah? How shall I set thee as Zeboim? Mine heart is turned within me; my repentings are kindled together." Let me take courage, then, and say that, mourning over the loss which He had sustained in being deprived of man's affection and obedience, He yearned in eager earnestness for his recovery. We can only speak of Deity in human words, and these must lose some of their earthly meaning when applied to Him. Nevertheless, it standeth here most sure, that God, when man sinned, lost that which He very much desired to retain; and that the weight of this loss impelled Him to seek after human salvation. In the consciousness of loss, there-

fore, on Jehovah's part, the great work of redemption began. " He *so* loved the world, that
he gave his only begotten Son." What is that
but just another way of saying, He so missed
man's affection and fellowship, that He gave His
only begotten Son? He sought our salvation,
not only for our sakes, but for His own ; and thus
the sense of loss out of which sprang the purpose of recovering the sinner corresponds, at the
one end of the chain, with the rapturous joy that
is felt at the other, when " the ransomed of the
Lord return, and come to Zion." This view of
the matter may well give careless sinners food
for serious reflection. You are God's. By virtue of your very creaturehood you belong to
Him. Your hearts, your lives, your service, ought
all to be given to Him ; but they are not, and
this is no mere thing of indifference to Him.
He misses you. He, on whom the universe
hangs, and who well might be excused if He had
no concern for you, misses your love. He hungers for your affection. He desires your return
to Him. Yea, he has used means of the most
costly character to find you out, and to bring you
back. Why will you continue to disregard Him?
Why will you perversely malign Him as one who

takes no interest in your welfare? Believe, me, you can give Him no higher joy than you will cause by your return to Him, while your repentance will secure unalloyed happiness to yourselves.

II. But, in the second place, we have here set before us *the sinner's own helplessness.* He is like a lost sheep. Now, while, as we have seen, this means that God has lost him, we must not forget that, on the other side of it, the analogy also bears that the sinner has lost himself. There are few more helpless creatures than a wandered sheep. It runs hither and thither, " bleating up the moor in weary dearth," if perchance it may see another of its species, or regain the footsteps of the flock ; while it is ever liable to be assailed by wild beasts, or to fall headlong over some rugged precipice, or into some fearful pit. It is within the bounds of possibility, indeed, that it may find its way back to the fold; but this is not probable, and usually it comes back only when it is brought back under the good shepherd's care. Now, what is all this but a picture of the sinner? Fretting at its enclosure, and longing for the freedom which he expects outside, he has left God's fold. He has gone on and on, farther and ever farther away from his Creator ; he has missed the way to happiness ; nor can he find a pathway back to that which he has left. More helpless than the sheep, he cannot by any possibility return unaidedly to God. He is like one groping in the dark, or like the little child that has lost itself in the busy, bustling streets of the crowded city. All he can do is to confess his helplessness, and to lift up his voice and weep. But this, alas ! is usually the very last thing he is willing to do. It is, comparatively speaking, an easy thing to convince the sinner of his guilt, but it is a hard matter to get him to own his helplessness. He will persist in attempting his own deliverance. He will seek to satisfy God's law for himself, and to find his own way back to happiness. The sheep will run to the shepherd when he appears, and welcome him as its helper, looking up in dumb gratitude into his face. But the sinner, in this respect more stupid even than the sheep, too often runs from the Shepherd, and will have none of His assistance. Let there be no such pride and waywardness among us, my brethren ; but recognizing in Jesus the Helper whom we need, let us yield ourselves up to Him,

willing to own our helplessness, if only we may
be borne in His loving arms to happiness and
heaven.

III. We have here, in the third place, *the
means used for the sinner's recovery.* " Doth He
not leave the ninety and nine in the wilderness,
and go after that which is lost, until he find it?
And when he hath found it, he layeth it on his
shoulders, rejoicing?" Many questions rise out of
these words which are more easily asked than
answered. Thus—Whom do these ninety and
nine represent? what is meant by the leaving
of them, and going after that which is lost? and
when may the lost be said to be truly found?
The ninety and nine are described (in the seventh
verse) as just persons which need no repentance.
Now, some have supposed that we have here a
reference to the Scribes and Pharisees, to whose
sneer we have before alluded. They would
make it an ironical expression of Christ's like
that other—" They that are whole need not a
physician, but they that are sick. I came not to
call the righteous, but sinners, to repentance;"
and they would interpret the leaving of the ninety
and nine, as a kind of implied vindication of

Himself, by Jesus, for leaving the Scribes and Pharisees, and going after the publicans and sinners. This gives a good and consistent enough meaning, and there are many reasons why I should be disposed to adopt it; yet two thoughts weigh with me in inclining me to prefer another. *First*, It is positively said here, that these ninety-nine need no repentance; therefore, it is implied that they have never sinned. *Second*, In the expression, " Joy shall be in heaven over one sinner that repenteth more than over ninety and nine just persons which need no repentance," it is evidently suggested that there is some joy over the ninety and nine. But this cannot be true if the ninety and nine represent the Scribes and Pharisees, since it is impossible to conceive that any inhabitant of heaven could rejoice over them. Hence, though even that interpretation is involved in many difficulties, I prefer to regard the ninety and nine as descriptive of the angels who have kept their first estate, and who ceaselessly serve God before His throne. If, then, this representation be correct, the leaving of the ninety and nine will signify the leaving of heaven by the Eternal Son, when at the era of the incarnation He set out in search of that which was lost;

and the search itself will include everything which Jesus did by His own personal ministry on earth, and by His sacrificial death upon the cross, and everything which He has done and is now doing, by the preaching of His ministers, and by the strivings of His spirit for the recovery of sinners. All the way from heaven to Calvary Jesus came to seek lost sinners. He died that the path might be opened up for Him to go further still in search of them, and for them to be brought righteously back under His loving care. He was going after that which was lost when He sat by the well of Sychar, and conversed with the woman of Samaria ; when he called Matthew in his toll-booth, and when he summoned Zacchæus from the branch of the sycamore-tree whereon he was perched. He was going after that which was lost when He shed forth His spirit upon Pentecost, and inspired His servants to proclaim His truth with power ; and He is still going after that which is lost, in the events of His providence, whereby He rouses the careless to reflection ; in the searching words of His earnest ministers, who stately declare His love, and speak home to the hearts of their fellow-men ; and in the strivings of His spirit, whereby, often when they can give no ac-

count of the matter, men's minds are strangely
turned in the direction of salvation. Yea, He is
going after that which is lost this morning, as,
once again, through the exposition of this parable,
His Love and earnestness, and tenderness, are
set before you ; nor will His search be concluded
until the day when the angel shall proclaim that
"Time shall be no longer." O! in view of
this unceasing work of the Good Shepherd,
may we not sing, in the words of the old
hymn,—

> " Wearily for me Thou soughtest ;
> On the cross my soul Thou boughtest ;
> Lose not all for which Thou wroughtest."

But when, it may be asked, is a sinner found by
Christ? The answer is, When, on his side, the
sinner finds Christ. The finding by Christ of the
lost sheep is, in the closing verse of the parable,
represented as the repenting of the sinner. When,
therefore, guilty and forlorn, without hope of acceptance in anything, save in the merits of his
Saviour, the sinner turns to God, he is found ;
or, borrowing a side-light from the third parable
here, when the prodigal comes to himself, and
says, " I will arise, and go to my father," at that

moment he is found by Christ. What is seen in
heaven is Christ laying His loving hand upon the
sinner, and the angels hear him, saying—" I have
found that which was lost;" but what is seen on
earth, is the sinner laying his believing hand on
Christ, and men hear him crying—" I have found
my deliverer. I will go with Him, for salvation is
with Him." But these are not two distinct
things—they are involved the one in the other,
so that you cannot take the one from the other
without destroying both. How they are thus
united we can no more tell than we can explain
how the soul resides in the body ; but the fact is
patent. Jesus lays hold of the lost soul at the
very moment when the sinner repents ; and so, if
you wish Him to be your Saviour, you must turn
in repentance from yourselves to Him, and give
up every hope of salvation save in Him.

But there is yet another aspect of this finding
which must in nowise be lost sight of. I mean
the tenderness of the shepherd. There is no
stroke of anger inflicted on the sheep, there is no
word of reproof addressed to it ; there is nothing but a soft caress, as, saying to it the while,
" poor thing, how far you have wandered, and how
worn and weary you are," he lifts it upon his

shoulders, and carries it to the fold. So it is with
Jesus and the sinner. The Saviour casteth not
up to him his past iniquities. He doth not chide
nor scold. "He upbraideth not." He doth not
wound the penitent's heart by taunting reference
to his former guilt, but he receiveth him joyfully.
He lets "the dead past bury its dead." He forgets the past, and exults only in the happiness of
having recovered that which was lost. Or, as
the prophet Isaiah phrased it—"The bruised
reed he doth not break ; the smoking flax he
doth not quench." You need not be afraid of
Him, O sinner! He will receive you with delight, and treat you with the utmost gentleness.

IV. But I cannot conclude without referring,
even though it must be now in the briefest terms,
to *the joy manifested by God over the sinner's
return.* "And when he cometh home, he calleth
together his friends and neighbors, saying unto
them, Rejoice with me ; for I have found my
sheep which was lost. I say unto you, that likewise joy shall be in heaven over one sinner that
repenteth, more than over ninety and nine just
persons which need no repentance." The home-
coming here can hardly be identical with the

finding of the lost one. It must rather, I think, be understood of the introduction of the saved one into heaven, by Jesus, at the last. Yet the joy over him is not delayed till then, though at that moment it becomes higher than before. Let me illustrate. You have lost your child, and one of the most trusted members of your family has set out in search of her. He is long away, and weary days and weeks you wait for news. At length, however, there comes from the great city or the far off continent a telegram from the seeker saying that he has found his sister, and that he is making arrangements for bringing her home as soon as possible. Of course, the mere receipt of his message gives you joy ; but when, at length, your loved one is brought home, that joy is intensified by the consciousness that she is safe again in your embrace. Now, your gladness at the receipt of the telegram corresponds to the joy in heaven over the sinner's repentance, while your higher joy at the home-coming of your child is symbolical of the gladness which will be caused by the entrance into heaven of each new ransomed spirit. Nor need we wonder at this joy. It is over a successful enterprise. It is over the deliverance of another soul from ruin. It is over another added to the heavenly inhabitants. It is over another trophy of the Redeemer's power to save. It is over a fresh manifestation of the manifold wisdom of God.

But why should there be more joy over the repenting sinner than over the unfallen angels ? Because there is greater delight in the recovery of that which has been in danger, than in the possession of that which has never been imperilled. The mother knows this, as she looks with keenest interest on the child that has been drawn, like another Moses, from out the very river of death. The greater the peril we have encountered, the deeper the thrill of joy when we are brought safely through it.

There is much to interest in the new-built ship. As the crowds gather round to see her launched, they hold their breaths awhile, until she slips in safety down into the element whereon she is henceforth to ride, and then they rend the air with deafening cheers. That is joy—a true and real joy.

But suppose a steamship that has left the port of Liverpool to cross the Atlantic, has not been heard of for many days after the date of her expected arrival here. Twenty-five or thirty-five

days have gone, and still there are no tidings.
Underwriters refuse to take another risk upon
her. She is given up for lost, and the relatives
of those who were on board go mourning as
for the dead. As a forlorn hope, a government
steamer is sent out to cruise about, if haply she
may find the missing ship, and at length, when
all expectation of seeing her again had been
abandoned, the news is told throughout the city
that she has been telegraphed off Sandy Hook,
and is coming up the Narrows in tow of the
vessel which had gone to seek her. How eagerly would thronging multitudes crowd the
wharves to see her as she came in! How tears
would mingle with their very cheers, and the joy
would radiate out over all the land, calling forth
gratitude from every heart. That too would be
gladness, but oh how much deeper, more thrilling,
more intense than that which was over the vessel
newly launched. Let the illustration dimly shadow forth to you the greater joy that is in
heaven over a saved sinner, than over the ninety and nine who have never been imperilled.

Such a joy, O sinner, you may occasion there.
Repent, therefore, even now, and as the news is
told on high, a thrill of gladness will pour along

the ranks of the redeemed. The angelic hosts
will share in the delight, and God Himself will
own the rapture of the moment as he says,
" Rejoice with me, for this my son was dead and
is alive again ; he was lost and is found."

THE LOST COIN.

"Either what woman having ten pieces of silver, if she lose one piece, doth not light a candle, and sweep the house, and seek diligently till she find it?

"And when she hath found it, she calleth her friends and her neighbors together, saying, Rejoice with me ; for I have found the piece which I had lost.

"Likewise, I say unto you, there is joy in the presence of the angels of God over one sinner that repenteth."

LUKE, xv., 8-10.

THE LOST COIN.

THE illustrations of some teachers, drawn as they are from the most recondite walks of science, need more explanation than the truths which they are intended to elucidate. But it was not so with those employed by Jesus. With a true poet's eye, He saw the beauty and spiritual significance of the commonest things; and so the casual incidents of daily life, the ordinary objects of familiar observation, as well as the habitual occupations of the household and the farm, were introduced by Him into His discourses in such a way as to captivate the attention, instruct the intellects, and move the hearts of His hearers. Hence, over and above the spiritual truths which they were designed to expound, we have in many of His parables exact delineations of actual scenes in Eastern life; while in that which we have just read we have a most realistic description of just such an occurrence as might have happened last week in any of our own homes. Nothing that I could say could bring either this woman or her work more vividly before you ; and any attempt to paraphrase the language in which they are here described would only end in a weak and watery dilution of the original production. Leaving it, therefore, to speak for itself, let us proceed to its interpretation.

Like that which goes before it, and with which it is so closely connected, this parable was primarily intended to illustrate the fact, that there is joy in heaven over a repenting sinner, and so to reprove the Scribes and Pharisees for the scorn which they meant to express when they said of Jesus, "This man receiveth sinners, and eateth with them." It describes a loss, a search, a recovery, and a joy consequent thereon ; and in all these respects it is only a reproduction of the story of the bringing home of the lost sheep. But there are some things suggested here which did not come out in our treatment of the former parable, and to these we shall now restrict ourselves. They centre in these three things : the

thing lost, the means used for its recovery, and
the kind of joy consequent on its being found.

I. Look at the thing lost, and you will find several points of importance thereby suggested.

It was a coin. That is to say, it was not simply
a piece of precious metal, but that metal moulded
and minted into money, bearing on it the king's
image and superscription, and witnessing to his
authority wherever it circulated. You remember
how, when his enemies, seeking to entangle Jesus,
asked whether it were lawful to give tribute to
Cæsar or no, He requested to see a coin; and
when one had been produced, He said, Whose is
this image and superscription? They replied,
Cæsar's. Whereupon He said, Render unto Cæsar
the things which are Cæsar's, and to God the
things which are God's. Now, reading this parable in connection with that narrative, we think of
this coin as stamped with the king's image, and
designed not only for a medium of exchange, but
also for a testimony to the royalty and right of
him whose likeness was impressed upon it. What
a beautiful thing is a new piece of money! How
sharply cut are the letters which are imprinted on
it! how finely relieved the likeness of the monarch

and how clear and glittering its polished surface ! Can we fail to see in it a type of the human soul, when first it came, new-minted, from the Creator's hand ? It had enstamped upon it His image in knowledge, righteousness, and holiness, and was designed by Him to be a willing witness-bearer to the rightfulness of His authority and the legitimacy of His throne. He made man in His own image, after His own likeness ; and so it is not by any means a stretching of the figure here to see in this piece of money, as it was at first, a representation of the soul's original dignity.

But *the coin was lost,* and this suggests that in sinful man the image of his Maker has gone out of sight, and the great purpose of his being has been frustrated. For any good which the piece of money, so long as it was lost, did to its owner, or for any testimony which it gave to the authority of him whose image it bore, it might as well have been non-existent. And, similarly, the sinner does no good in the world ; he gives no glory to God ; he is of no service to God, so far, at least, as the promotion of His honor, and the acknowledgment of His authority, are concerned. Instead of obeying God, he positively dishonors Him ; and in those parts of his nature on which, more especially, God's image was impressed, he is emphatically lost to God. His intellect does not like to retain God in its knowledge ; his heart has estranged its love from God ; and his life is devoted to another lord than his Creator. He is lost.

Yet he is not absolutely worthless. *The coin though lost, has still a value.* If it can be recovered, it will be worth as much as ever. It may be blackened with rust, or soiled with mud or covered over with dust, but it is still silver— nay, it is still minted silver, with traces of the superscription and the image that gave it currency. Even so the human soul is valuable though lost. It has in it the silver of immortality ; and, depraved though it be, its intellectual powers, its moral freedom, its soaring ambition, and its upbraiding conscience, tell not only of its former grandeur, but also of its present importance. Even as he is, man is the most valuable being in the world. There is nothing equal to him, nothing almost which we can place second after him. There is a wide, yawning, impassable gulf between him and the highest of the lower animals. He has a dignity to which they can lay no claim. He has a character which is unique and peculiar to himself. In spite of "theories of development," and recent perverse efforts on the part of some to claim kindred with the ape, there is in every human being a moral consciousness that marks him man, and not brute, together with such feelings after the future life as stamp him immortal; and this is the silver of the coin that once bore the distinct and well-defined lineaments of Jehovah's image.

But yet, again, *this coin was lost in the house.* The woman did not let it fall as she was crossing the wild and trackless moor, neither did she drop it into the unfathomed depths of ocean. Had she done so, she would never have thought of seeking for it; she would have given it up as irrecoverable. But, knowing that it fell from her in the house, and, therefore, that it must have rolled away somewhere within its walls, she set about a vigorous search, sure that it could be found. Now, this points to the fact that the soul of the sinner is recoverable. It is capable of being restored to its original dignity and honor. It has in it still, potentialities as great and glorious as those which ever belonged to it. There are many things which cannot be renewed. No hu-

man alchemy can bleach into its original white-
ness the blackened snow which has been trodden
into miry slush upon the city streets ; no artistic
ingenuity can replace upon the peach the downy
softness of its skin when you have rubbed it off
upon the ragged wall ; no manufacturing skill can
restore to the violet the velvet softness of its leaf
after it has been once crumpled up into many
folds ; but the soul of man, even in its most be-
sotted and depraved condition, is capable of being renewed, and may yet become a pure and
holy denizen of the heavenly home. For " Who
are these in white robes ? and whence came they ?
They have washed their robes, and made them
white in the blood of the Lamb ;" they are souls
renewed by the power of God's Spirit through
the work of His Son. This lost coin, then, has
a past history behind it, and a future capability
before it. Its past history bids us despise no fel-
low-man, since, no matter what may be the color
of his skin, or the complexion of his character,
there are yet traces of his old dignity upon
him, letters of the superscription that once told
whose image was impressed upon him. Its future capability bids us despair of no individual
sinner ; for though he be lost to all that is no-

ble, and lovely, and holy, and divine, there is a possibility of his recovery. The coin has not fallen into the dark inaccessible mountain ravine, nor into the depths of the unfathomed sea, but it has gone amissing in the house, and so it may be found. The lost sinner may be recovered. Go, then, ye whom Christ has found, and seek him ; nor count any labor too great, or any sacrifice too costly, if only you may be able to add another gem to the Redeemer's crown.

II. This brings me to the consideration of the search, wherein we have also some things suggested which are peculiar to this parable. Eastern houses are constructed in such a way as to keep out the light and heat of the sun as much as possible. They have few windows, and even the few which they have are shaded with such lattice-work as tends to exclude, rather than admit, the sunbeam. Hence the rooms are generally dark ; and so, even if the coin were lost at noonday, the light of a candle would be required to seek for it.

Nor was there, in Eastern dwellings, the same scrupulous cleanliness that we love to see in many homes among ourselves. The floors were often covered with rushes, which, being changed only at rare intervals, collected a vast amount of dust and filth, among which a piece of money might be most readily lost. Hence the lighting of a candle and the sweeping of the house were the most natural things to be done in such a case.

But whom does this woman represent? and what, spiritually, are we to understand by the lighting of a candle and the sweeping of the house? The woman, in my judgment, symbolizes the Holy Spirit. Mr. Arnot, indeed, in his valuable work upon the Parables, says that this view is untenable, alleging that, since the shepherd who lost the sheep represents the Lord Jesus Christ, the woman who lost the coin must represent Him too. But if this reasoning be worth anything, we must carry it further still, and affirm that the father who lost the son in the next parable represents the Lord Jesus. This, however, would be to contradict the uniform tenor of the interpretation of that matchless story in all ages; for every reader of it, not to say every writer on it, understands the earthly parent to typify and illustrate our Father who is in heaven. If, therefore, in the

third parable, the loser is God the Father, and
not the Lord Jesus Christ, we see no inconsis-
tency in maintaining that the woman here must
be understood as representing the Holy Spirit.
Nay, rather, there is to our thinking a beauty
and completeness in this interpretation that all
others lose. That which was lost, whether we
call it sheep, or coin, or son, was lost by the
Godhead, and in these three parables we have
brought before us a part, at least, of the work
and office of each of the three Persons in the
great plan of redemption. We took the leaving
of the ninety-nine sheep in the wilderness, and
the going after that which was lost, to signify
the incarnation of Christ and all to which it
led; we shall take the prodigal's reception by
his father to illustrate God's manner of welcoming a returning sinner; and so, naturally, we understand the woman here to represent the Holy
Spirit; and we look upon the means which she
employed in her search for the lost coin as denoting the efforts made by the Holy Spirit for
the recovery of a lost soul.

Now let us see what these were. She light-
ed a candle, and swept the house, and searched
diligently. The light most evidently represents

the truth; but what are we to make of the sweeping? Some would take it to illustrate the purifying work of the Holy Ghost in the heart. But that view cannot be maintained, since the purifying of the soul is not a work in order to, but rather subsequent upon, its first recovery. I take it rather, therefore, to represent that disturbance of settled opinions and practices—that turning of the soul, as it were, upside down—which is frequently seen as a forerunner of conversion; that confusion and disorder occasioned by some providential dealing with the man, such as personal illness, or business difficulties, or family bereavement, or the like, and which frequently issues in the coming of the soul to God; for here also chaos often precedes creation. Truth introduced into the heart, and providential disturbances and unsettlements in order to its introduction—these are the things symbolized by the lighting of the candle and the sweeping of the house.

The truth which the Holy Spirit employs for the purpose of conversion is the Word of God, all of which has been given to men by His own inspiration; and the special portion of that Word which He uses for His saving work is the, wondrous story of the cross. "The truth as it is in Jesus"—the fact that "God so loved the world that he gave his only-begotten Son, that whosoever believeth in Him should not perish, but have everlasting life"—the faithful saying, that "Christ Jesus came into the world to save sin·ners;"—this is the light which He employs. No new revelations does He now bestow. He uses still this old gospel—the good news of salvation through Him who died for our offences, and rose again for our justification. In one word, the truths which centre in the cross of Calvary, are those which the Spirit employs in the conversion of men. It was so on the day of Pentecost; it has been so in every period of true spiritual revival; it has been so in every individual conversion. They say that in some of our large millinery establishments many needles are lost in the course of the day; and that in seeking to recover them, instead of going down upon the carpet and wearifully picking each one up, a young woman goes round at night, holding a magnet near the floor, attracting thereby every minutest particle of steel, and so recovering all. So, in seeking to regain lost souls, the Holy Spirit goes through the world employing the mag-

net of the cross; everywhere, He seeks to draw
men to Himself by the attraction of its love,
and constrains them to live by the faith of Him
who loved them and gave Himself for them.

But not all at once do men attend to, and believe, this truth of the gospel. The magnet will
operate wherever there are no neutralizing ele-
ments near; but while the soul is sunk in depra-
vity, or engaged in worldly pursuits, or absorbed
in earthly pleasures, it feels not the charm of the
Redeemer's love. Hence means must be used to
destroy the counter-attractions of the world,
which keep men from God. Or, taking the figure
of my text, if the light of the candle fall immediately upon the coin, the seeker will at once pick
it up; but if the piece of money have dropped on
a rush-covered floor, and lie concealed beneath
the straw and the débris of weeks, these must be
removed before the rays of the candle can reveal
the coin. That is to say, in plainer language,
men do not usually attend to the truth at once.
They are pre-occupied with business; they are
engrossed in other things, and the Bible remains
beside them unread; the good news of the gospel are uncared-for and unbelieved. But then
comes the sweeping of the house. There are pro-

vidential disturbances in business; or there are family bereavements; or there is personal sickness; or there is the awakening of conscience to a sense of guilt, by the hearing of some solemn discourse, or, as the result of some other of the manifold expedients which God the Holy Spirit can employ, there is a general upturning of the soul, like the confusion that is created in the home by the annual house-cleaning; and just as, at these yearly lustrations, a great many things, which had been neglected for a long while, come forth into prominence, and compel you to settle what you will do with them; so, in the soul's disturbance, the long-buried questions about sin and salvation come up, and the man begins to cry, *What must I do to be saved?* Then as some Evangelist by his side exclaims, "*Believe in the Lord Jesus Christ, and thou shalt be saved,*" he turns in faith to Jesus; and that moment, the candle's beams falling upon the piece which was lost, the Holy Spirit finds and rejoices over the recovered soul.

You see then, the meaning of this seeking and sweeping: every time you are brought face to face with trial; every providential unsettlement that comes upon you; or, to use Jeremiah's ex-

pression, every " emptying out from vessel to vessel " to which you are subjected, is a new sweeping of the house by the Holy Spirit seeking for
the recovery of your soul. Has He sought you
yet in vain ? Oh, let him seek so no longer ; but
through this discourse, describing to you your individual history and circumstances, and quickening anew your conscience, let Him find you now,
as with devout repentance you exclaim, " Lord, I
believe ; help thou mine unbelief !"

III. We come now, in the third place, to look
at the joy over the recovered coin ; and here, as
before, we shall restrict ourselves to that which is
peculiar to this parable. In the story of the lost
sheep, while the social character of the joy is certainly referred to, the specialty in the gladness of
the shepherd over its finding lay in the fact, to
which prominence is given in the appended note
of interpretation, that it was greater than over
the ninety and nine which had never strayed.
Here, however, the peculiarity is in the sociality
of the joy. The woman, when she had found
her money, " called together her friends and neighbors, saying, Rejoice with me ; for I have found
the piece which I had lost." This is peculiarly

true to Eastern life. Even to this day, as I have
been informed by one who is well acquainted
with the domestic habits of the people of Pales-
tine, the jewels of a Syrian woman consist for
the most part of pieces of money. They are her
own exclusive property. which her husband may not
claim, and having descended to her as heirlooms
from her mother, they are handed down by her to
her daughters. They are commonly worn tied in
the hair, the larger pieces generally hanging from
the ends of the braids. Thus one falling out of
the hair, might be very readily lost; while as it
formed a part of the dowry of the woman, in
which all her descendants had an interest as well
as she, we can easily see how its loss and recovery would be almost equally affecting to them
all. It was quite natural, therefore, for an Eastern
woman to call for her female friends to rejoice
with her over the finding of one of her treasured
heirlooms. But gladness everywhere is diffusive.
We cannot have the highest kind of joy if we must
keep it to ourselves. There are certain sorrows
which must find vent in tears, else death will ensue
to the individual ; and in this connection every one
remembers the words in Tennyson's fine song,
"She must weep, or she will die." But there is

the same thing at the other extremity. There are joys which, if we may not utter them, cease to be joys, and which, if we cannot share them with others, will seriously injure ourselves. The pent-up emotion will choke us ; but the utterance of it to others, and the making of them partakers of our gladness, renders it safe for us, and in the end not only makes them happier, but makes our own hearts more joyful. Every reader of ancient history remembers the *Heureka* of Archimedes; and each individual can tell of times in his own experience when, eager for an opportunity to utter his gladness, he has gone long miles to make it known to those, who, he knew, would be sure to rejoice with him.

But, in this respect, man is but the far-off image of God. His joy also, if I may dare to use the words, needs society to make it complete; and the fact that there are those beside Him to whom He can make known the story of each recovered soul, redoubles His own gladness, and diffuses among them His own divine delight. We know not, indeed, with certainty, who these are in heaven, who are here symbolized by the friends and neighbors of the woman—whether they be the unfallen angels, or pure beings, summoned from other worlds, that they may hear the marvellous history which centres in this planet, earth; but, whoever they may be, they enter into the feelings of the Most High, and the utterance of their congratulations is the occasion of the highest happiness of Deity. Nor let it be supposed that this is a mere fanciful idea, for which there is no foundation in Scripture apart from the teaching of this parable. What says Paul—"God hath created all things by Jesus Christ: to the intent that now, unto the principalities and powers in heavenly *places*, might be known through the Church the manifold wisdom of God." (Eph. iii. 10.) Now, these words mean, if they mean anything at all, that through the Church, God designed to show to principalities and powers in heavenly places His manifold wisdom. In the manifestation of this wisdom God has His highest work, and, in its appreciation by spiritual intelligences, through the Church of Christ, He has His greatest joy. Farther than this I dare not go; but up to this point we must advance, if at least we would rightly interpret this delightful parable.

Now, strictly speaking, my present work is done. I have shown you as clearly and succinctly as possible, what I judge to be the special teachings of this story; but I cannot conclude without giving prominence to two thoughts which may be of some practical value to us all.

In the first place I remind you of the possibility of the recovery of any soul. There is no one one beyond hope. No sinner need despair of himself, and no worker in the service of Jesus need despair of the conversion of any one for whose recovery he is ardently praying and earnestly working. However depraved or degraded a man may be, he is not beyond hope so long as the truth of the Gospel may be proclaimed in his hearing. I cannot put this thought more strikingly than it has been presented in the following lines, selected from the poem entitled " Beautiful Snow," especially when they are read in the light of the interesting history which has been told, with what truth I know not, in connection with them. " In the early part of the American war, one dark Saturday morning, there died in the Commercial Hospital, Cincinnati, a young woman, over whose head only two and twenty summers had passed. She had once been possessed of an enviable share of beauty ; but, alas! upon her fair brow had long been

written the terrible word, Fallen. Among her
personal effects was found, in manuscript, the
" Beautiful Snow," which was immediately car-
ried to a gentleman of culture and literary taste,
who was at that time Editor of the " National
Union." In the columns of that paper, on the
morning following the girl's death, the poem appeared in print for the first time." It is all ex-
quisite, but for my present purpose, I give only
these three verses :

   *   •   •   •   •   •   •

> Once I was pure as the snow, but I fell,
> Fell like the snow, but from heaven to hell ;
> Fell to be trampled, as filth of the street ;
> Fell to be scoffed, to be spit on, and beat ;
>   Pleading,—cursing,—dreading to die,
> Selling my soul to whoever would buy ;
> Dealing in shame for a morsel of bread ;
> Hating the living, and fearing the dead.
> Merciful God ! Have I fallen so low ?
> And yet I was once like the beautiful snow !
>
> Once I was fair as the beautiful snow,
> With an eye like a crystal, a heart like its glow ;
> Once I was loved for my innocent grace—
> Flattered and sought for the charms of my face !
>   Father,—mother,—sisters,—all,
> God and myself I have lost by my fall ;
> The veriest wretch that goes shivering by

Will make a wide sweep, lest I wander too nigh ;
For all that is on or about me I know,
There is nothing that's pure as the beautiful snow.

*   *   *   *   *   *   *

Helpless and foul as the trampled snow,
Sinner, despair not ! Christ stoopeth low
To rescue the soul that is lost in sin,
And raise it to life and enjoyment again.
    Groaning,—bleeding,—dying, for thee,
The Crucified hung on the cursed tree !
His accents of pity fall soft on thine ear.
" Is there mercy for me? Will He heed my weak prayer ?
O God ! in the stream that for sinners did flow
Wash me ! and I shall be whiter than snow."

Take to thyself, O sinner, the message of these
lines, and make for thyself the prayer with which
they conclude. No matter how aggravated thine
iniquities have been, or how deeply depraved thy
spirit may be, there is mercy for thee. Thou
mayest yet be forgiven and renewed, if only thou
wilt trust in Him who is " able to save unto the
uttermost all that come unto God by Him."

Finally, let me once more insist upon the truth,
that the most God-like work in which any one
can engage is that of seeking to save the lost.
Look, again, at the teachings of this chapter. In
the first parable we have the Divine Son, the

Good Shepherd, coming into the world after the lost sheep; in the second, as we have just seen, we have the Divine Spirit putting forth His agency for the recovery of sinful souls; and, in the third, we have the Divine Father welcoming, in the fullness of infinite tenderness, the returning penitent. Are we wrong, then, when from these things we deduce the inference, that the great work and happiness of Godhead are connected with the salvation of lost souls? But if this be so, it will follow that man is then likest God, and most really a partaker of His happiness, when He is seeking to save the lost. Do you want to be, in the highest sense, a fellow-laborer with God? do you wish to be a sharer of the loftiest joy which even Deity can know? Then go forth to seek and to save that which was lost. Care not what sacrifices it may involve, or what discomforts it may entail upon you. Never mind, though it may require you to go to dens of infamy or haunts of sin. These are not so far beneath you as this evil world was beneath the Eternal Son of God; neither are they anything like so far removed from your refinement of nature, as this world was from His infinite purity. Go, and He will take care of you, and give you success. Were some fashionable lady to drop her diamond ring into the gutter, she would not scruple to thrust her ungloved hand into the filthy sewage, if thereby she might recover her precious ornament ; and shall not we expose ourselves, if need be, to contact with moral and spiritual impurity, if only we may be instrumental in recovering the immortal jewel of a human soul, and restoring it to its Creator's hand ? The great novelist has no more touching or pathetic chapter in his voluminous writings than that which tells how the big, burly, honest sailor set out from his boat-house on the Yarmouth shore, to seek for her who had been ruined by the villain whom he took to be his friend ; and when we shall feel about lost sinners as he did about her ; when we shall go forth in a search for them as earnest, as long, and as persistent as was his, we shall begin to be disciples indeed, and shall know something of the joy that is in heaven over one sinner that repenteth. Earth has no happiness like to his who is instrumental in finding the piece that was lost, and restoring it to its Heavenly Owner. May God give us more of this celestial happiness !

THE PRODIGAL SON.

I.

THE DEPARTURE.

" And he said, A certain man had two sons :

" And the younger of them said to his father, Father, give me the portion of goods that falleth to me. And he divided unto them his living.

" And not many days after, the younger son gathered all together, and took his journey into a far country, and there wasted his substance with riotous living.

" And when he had spent all, there arose a mighty famine in that land ; and he began to be in want.

" And he went and joined himself to a citizen of that country ; and he sent him into his fields to feed swine.

" And he would fain have filled his belly with the husks that the swine did. eat ; and no man gave unto him."

LUKE, xv., 11-16.

THE PRODIGAL SON.

I.

THE DEPARTURE.

NOT without many misgivings do I venture on the exposition of this parable. It is in itself so perfect, as holding up the mirror to nature, that I am afraid to touch it, lest I should dim its surface by defiling fingers ; and its main teachings are so clearly defined, that I fear lest, in seeking to explain and enforce them, I should prove to be like that commentator on the "Pilgrim's Progress" whose notes were harder to be understood than the original allegory. Nevertheless, as it is a necessary appendix to, and completion of, the truth portrayed in those which I have already considered, I am constrained to enter upon its examination ; and my prayer is, that the Spirit of Him who spake it may rest upon me while I seek to illustrate it, and may keep me from saying anything that may mar its force, overlay its beauty, or destroy its pathos.

Like those by which it is preceded, it was designed to rebuke the cold-hearted and self-righteous exclusiveness of the Scribes and Pharisees, and to show them that, in despising Jesus for receiving sinners and eating with them, they were altogether out of harmony with Him who rejoiceth over one sinner that repenteth. But it differs from them in that, while they illustrate the manner in which God seeks the lost sinner, it describes the result of that search in the voluntary return of the sinner himself. They view the matter from the Divine side, and let us see the efforts which God has put forth in the incarnation of His Son, and the agency of His Spirit, to find and save that which has been lost. This regards the subject from the human side, and shows us the sinner rising from his degradation and returning to his Father. Yet they are not so much two separate and distinct things, as two sides of one and the same thing. Admirably has Mr. Arnot said here, " It is not that some of fallen human kind are saved after the manner of the strayed sheep, and others after the manner of the prodigal son ;

not that the Saviour bears one wanderer home by His power, and that another of his own accord arises and returns to the Father. Both these processes are accomplished in every conversion. The man comes, yet Christ brings him ; Christ brings him, yet he comes." The Spirit sweeps the house and finds him ; yet he himself of his own free choice arises and goes to his Father.

Again, in the two preceding parables, little or nothing is said as to the sinner's departure from God, and his misery and degradation in his lost condition. The main points which they illustrate are the seeking, the finding, and the joy resulting from the recovery. The loss which they describe is rather a loss sustained, if I may so say, by Deity ; and scarcely any hint is given of that which is incurred by the sinner himself. Here, however, the misery of man away from God, and in the far land of sin, is set in the forefront ; and nowhere in the whole range of literature, whether sacred or profane, have we a more vivid exemplification of the awful truth, that " the way of transgressors is hard."

In the episode of the elder brother, too, we have something unique and peculiar to this parable. In the former allegories there is no jarring or dissonant note in the chorus of rejoicing over the recovery of that which was lost; but here, that in the mirror which Jesus held up, the Scribes and Pharisees might see their own likeness as well as His, we have one surly and sour dissentient, who virtually says to his Father, what they had said to Jesus, " Wilt thou receive a sinner and eat with him ?"

But, without lingering longer on the mere outlines of the story, let us look at the incidents which it records. We are introduced into a family whose home, for anything that appears to the contrary, may have been in some sweet rural retreat, with every added accessory of comfort and enjoyment. There is a father and two grown-up sons, and for a time all is happiness and harmony. But at length, weary of the monotony of the country ; or chafing under the sense of restraint which the father's presence created ; or moved by that spirit of adventure and desire to see life and the world, which most lads feel in the opening days of manhood ; or perhaps wishing merely to do for himself, to make his own way, and to secure his own independence, the younger son desires to go away.

He has talked of it often before, but his mother has always won him over by her affection; and for her sake he has consented to stay yet awhile. Now, however, the fever is in his veins again. Go he must, and shall. So, as the less of two evils, his father gives him a proper outfit, and in the most handsome manner, anticipating the division of his property that would be made in any case at his death, he bestows upon him his portion. The farewells are soon said, and away he goes. He is bound for a far land—the El Dorado of his dreams, where money is to be made, and greatness is to be achieved, and whence, perchance, he hopes to return, in the evening of his days, a nabob, rolling in wealth, the envy of every beholder. That was the ideal before him; but, ah!- how different was the reality; when he reached his destination, indeed, everything looked bright, and it was his intention to do well. Had anybody then lifted the veil of the future, and shown him himself as he was so soon to be, all tattered and filthy, in the swine-herd's den, he would have shrunk back aghast, and shuddered as he cried, " Impossible!" And, doubtless, if it had required only a single step to bring him to that degradation, that single step would never have been taken. But thus in all likelihood it happened. He became connected with evil companions; they led him gradually into wicked courses; and so long as he had money to spend with them, they were assiduous in their attentions, and superlative in their flattery. When, however, his means ran done they left him to himself. Famine arose, and, to keep himself from starvation, he went and joined himself to—or, as the words might perhaps be better rendered, he glued* himself to, or, he fastened himself, upon—a wealthy citizen, who sent him to herd his swine; and such was the extremity to which he was reduced, that he would gladly have fed from the trough from which they ate, or on the pods of the carob-tree by which they were fattened.

Think that to a Jew the swine was an unclean, abhorred animal, and then you will have some faint idea of the degradation which, in the estimation of His hearers, Jesus here portrays. But have we nothing like this in our own land, and in our own day? Who has not known some youth who has come from the country to one of our

---

* The old Scotch word to "sorn" upon one, seems to me to be the exact equivalent of the original here.

large towns, and gone through just such a career?
He has left behind him a pious father and a praying mother, and come with high hopes of success
in life to some of our great offices, that he may fit
himself for after eminence. But his fellows
laugh at his countrified manners, and ridicule
what they call his old-fashioned scruples, until, at
length, weary of their scorn, and worn out by
their importunity, he goes with them to their
haunts of sin. He learns to like strong drink,
and quaffs his beer at every hour of the day. He
frequents the theatre, and counts it a high honor
to have the *entrée* into the green-room, and to be
on terms of familiality with those who act upon
the stage. He is easily led on after all this to
lascivious indulgence; or, mayhap, he keeps his
betting-book, and begins to talk oracularly about
this or that "event;" but when the settling-day
comes round, he finds that he has hopelessly involved himself in debts, misnamed of honor,
which he cannot meet. His master's money is at
his command, and his emergency constitutes an
apparent necessity, which he does not care to
resist. He uses that with which for other pur-
poses he had been entrusted. He absconds; is
hunted by detectives, and, hemmed round by tel-

egraphic wires on every side, he is soon appre-
hended and brought back, like Eugene Aram,
"with gyves upon his wrists." Then, after standing in the prisoner's dock, disgraced in the very
city in which he had dreamed of winning honor,
he is led away to the degradation of the peni-
tentiary, or the drudgery of convict labor.   Or, if
the issue be not such as I have described, it may
be something equally repulsive.   He may become
a habitual drunkard, sacrificing everything to an
abominable appetite ; or, worse even than that, he
may develop into a contemptible "black-leg,"
preying upon the unsuspicious, and making himself jackal to some gambling haunt, until, at
length, stabbed in some deadly quarrel, or mad-
dened by the delirium of intemperance, he goes
to his own place, unwept, save by the mother,
who, hearing of the tragedy in her far-off home,
wrings her hands, and cries, "O my son! my
son! would God I had died for thee! my son!
my son!"   For remember, it is not every prodigal's history that has the issue of this parable,
and in many, many instances the grave comes
only to cover, with its dark green pall, the more
dreadful experiences that lie beyond.   It may
seem, indeed, aside from the main line of spirit-

ual exposition to dwell upon such things as these; and strictly speaking, so it is. But I am looking now at the parable, not as an allegory, but as a literal narrative which it may well enough have been. And it is not aside from my mission as a minister, especially in a large community like this, to bring out strongly and broadly the danger of such practices as those to which I have alluded. I might fortify my remarks, and vindicate the dark picture which I have drawn, by many sad examples taken from the records of our various courts ; but I prefer to give you one or two cases which have passed under my own observation. I have seen, sitting shoeless and shirtless on a cab, ' joining himself to ' the driver, if haply he might get anything out of him, a young man who had inherited a large fortune, who had been in the same classes with me at school, and who had sat as a student for the ministry on the same benches with me at College. I have visited in a Liverpool prison where he was under sentence of six months' imprisonment for stealing a watch, which he had pawned for drink, a man who was an M.A. of a Scottish University, and who had been Principal of a College in a foreign land. I have had, as a beggar at my door, a man of my own age, brought up in the same street with me, who had squandered a large patrimony in such courses as I have described; and as I saw the grey hair of his premature old age streaming in the wind, and heard him call me by the old familiar name of my boyhood, as he besought me for assistance, I could not but think of these words, "And when he had spent all, there arose a mighty famine in the land, and he began to be in want."

Similar cases, I feel confident, have been witnessed by almost all before me who have attained to middle life; and with such occurrences in my remembrance, I cannot allow the present opportunity to pass without uttering a few words of warning to those young people here who have only recently left the home of their childhood for the life of the great city, or who have passed from the routine of the school, to the stir, and activity, and temptations of modern business.

Two things I would especially urge:

Beware of evil companions. Wait till you see what is in men before you trust yourselves to them. Do not allow yourselves to be led away by appearances. Soft speeches, flattering words, a winning manner, and an artless way, may all be assumed only the better to decoy you. Distrust all those who would ridicule to you the sanctity and associations of home. Have no confidence in any one who would endeavor to shake your faith in the Scriptures, or attempt to lead you away from the observance of the Sabbath, and the enjoyment of the sanctuary. Do not permit yourselves to be moved from your convictions by the swagger or the ridicule of any one. Have faith in God, have faith in yourself, and cultivate the friendship of those only who are the friends of Jesus. Seek to find friends in the church. Call upon and cultivate the acquaintance of your minister. Lay yourself out for work in connection with the congregation which you wish to join, and thus you will find resources for the spending of those leisure hours which have so much to do with making or marring the life-history of every man. I know that you will say, in response to all this, " Yes, it is very good ; but then congregations are so exclusive that one may attend a church regularly for months, and no one speak to him." Now, to a certain extent, I admit the truth of your words ; and I would say to the members of this church, that it is a sacred duty which they owe to Jesus, to show interest in all who come thus, strangers and unbefriended, into the midst of us.

Who can tell but that some youth, who has been worshipping here for weeks, and has since gone into evil courses, might have been led upwards instead, if some of us had only taken him by the hand? When your own children go away from you to a strange place, you will count it the highest favor that could be shown to you if some Christian friend will but open his heart to them. As ye would, therefore, that men should do to you, do ye even so now to them; and, for the sake of the parents who are praying far away, show kindness to the children, who are strangers here. But while I frankly admit the exclusiveness of modern church life, and bitterly bewail it, I would say also to my young friend who is a stranger, There may be a good deal of the same exclusiveness in yourself. If you make no advances, you can scarcely wonder if no advances are made to you; and, in general, I am sure of this, that if you will only offer your services for Christian work, and get in among the active people in the church—in Sunday-school operations, or in those of any of the other associations—you will soon feel yourself at home. Your heart will get a local centre, and you will become so interested in higher things that the temptations of the city will cease to charm you.

But, as a second advice, I would say, Beware of evil habits. Easily learned, they are most difficult to be overcome. At first slender as "the spider's most attenuated thread," they thicken round us into cords by which we are bound into the most utter helplessness. No slavery may for one moment be compared to that of the man who is the servant of his lusts, and the victim of pernicious habits. Withstand beginnings, therefore. "Look not on the wine when it is red in the cup." nor let your strength be eaten out of you by its bewitching influence. There is a coiled adder at the bottom of the steaming bowl, and, however it may be concealed at first, it will "at the last" sting you into spiritual death. Hear the confession of one of the finest of English Essayists, who unhappily knew from experience only too well the degradation which he describes, and take the warning which he cries to you out of his depths: "The waters have gone over me. But out of the black depths, could I be heard, I would cry to all those who have but set a foot in the perilous flood. Could the youth to whom the flavor of his first wine is delicious as the opening scenes of life, or the entering upon some newly-discovered Paradise, look into my desolation, and be made to understand what a dreary thing it is when a man shall feel himself going down a precipice with open eyes and a passive will; to see his destruction, and have no power to stop it, and yet to feel it all the way emanating from himself; to perceive all goodness emptied out of him, and yet not be able to fix a time when it was otherwise; to bear about the piteous spectacle of his own self-ruin; could he see my fevered eye, feverish with last night's drinking, and feverishly-looking for this night's repetition of the folly; could he feel the body of the death out of which I cry hourly with feebler and feebler outcry to be delivered,—it were enough to make him dash the sparkling beverage to the earth in all the pride of its mantling temptation—to make him clasp his teeth,

'And not undo them,
To suffer wet damnation to run through them.'"*

Alas! poor Lamb; may thy words to-day prove words of power to every one of us!

But intemperance is not the only evil habit of

---

* See Essays of Elia : The Confessions of a Drunkard.

which you need to have a care. Flee youthful
lusts. Keep yourselves pure ; for sensuality, too,
lays a deep hold upon the man, and drags him
down to utter loathsomeness. One who spake
from his own life-history has said regarding it,
that it " hardens a' within, and petrifies the feeling." It poisons the imagination of a man, cor-
rupts his heart, and depraves his entire nature ;
so that though he may, to the shame of all society, retain his place in the most fashionable circles,
and be courted by parents for the daughters of
their home, the sensualist is ever the most selfish
of mortals, having the passions of an animal,
while the conscience which should restrain them
is hardened into insensibility and impotence.

Be on your guard, too, against the seductions
of gambling. Do not bet even " the thousandth
part of one poor scruple " upon any event,
whether it be the issue of a game, or the winning
of a race, or the rolling of a ball. Say not to me
that you do so only for a small amount : the principle is the same, whether the stake be a cent or
a thousand dollars. It is by littles that the habit
is acquired ; yet when it has obtained the mas-
tery I question if there be one other passion
which so absorbs and overpowers the soul as that

of betting ; and in these days, when among the
" old nobility " of Great Britain the fortunes of
dukedoms and the estates of earls have been gam-
bled away ; when the youth of our commercial
cities are staking right and left upon politicians
and pugilists, and upon dogs and horses, and
when even in our exchanges so much of what is
called business is as really gambling as anything
you will see at Homburg or Wiesbaden, it is surely time to call a halt. Go not, I beseech you,
in these ways of iniquity : the gate may be wide,
the path may be flowery, and, for a time, prosperity may seem to attend you ; but it leads down-
ward, and its end is death. Enter not through the
gate, therefore, but " stand ye in the ways, and
see, and ask for the old paths, where is the good
way, and walk therein, and ye shall find rest unto
your souls."

Thus far I have been dealing with this story
as if it were only a literal narrative ; and I could
not, with any justice to my own feelings, or any
proper fidelity to you, withhold from you the
lessons which, even from this aspect of it, we may
learn. But we should greatly mistake its meaning if we should restrict its reference to those who
are accounted prodigals by their fellow-men. It

has a spiritual significance underlying its external incidents ; and, thus viewed, every man is a prodigal. God is the Father whom we have left ; sin is the far land into which we have wandered ; and the famine pictured in these verses is but a faint delineation of the spiritual desolation to which we have reduced ourselves by our iniquity. This, which is the interpretation proper of the first portion of the parable, I will try to put before you briefly ere I close.

I. Here is, first, *the nature of sin*. It is a departure from our Heavenly Father—a determination to be independent of God—a taking of the ordering of our lives into our own hands—a chafing under the restraints alike of the Divine law and the Divine love, and a setting up of ourselves as our own gods. Cunningly did Satan say to our common parents at the first—" Ye shall be as God, knowing good and evil ;" and still this self-assertion lies at the root of our alienation of heart from God, and rebellion of life against Him.

But yet more, this alienation of heart is from a Father ; this rebellion is against One who has done more for us than ever mother did for the son of her love. I know no more touching exposition of God's Fatherhood than that which this parable furnishes. Some, indeed, will have it that not until Jesus was revealed as the eternal Son, did God declare Himself the Father of any one in our human nature. But this opinion will not stand before such a parable as that which we are now considering. I willingly allow that only through Jesus Christ does God now, consistently with His personal honor and righteous administration, receive sinners back again as sons into His home. But surely, in the relationship between the prodigal and his father, here, we have a type of that which existed between God and man before the fall. If this be not so, then, for any significance that lies in the phrase, you might as well have read, "A certain king had two subjects;" or "A certain master had two servants." But if you so read, you take away the whole pith and pathos of the story. Hence we cannot but think that here we have a reference to God's original fatherly relationship to the human race. Now this, while it explains why He was so anxious to get His lost children back, and gives them such a welcome when they do return, does also, from the other side of it, deepen the guilt of the

sinner. His offence is not merely that of disobedience to a master, or treason against a king, but
it is, in combination with both of these, ingratitude to a Father. We condemn, as the most cul-
pable of all things, the cruelty of a son to his
venerable parent : and we have scarcely language
strong enough to express our detestation of such
conduct as that of Absalom to his father. Yet, in
God's sight, we have been doing the very same
thing, and we have given him occasion to say
concerning us, as Israel of old, "Hear, O heav-
ens, and give ear, O earth ; for the Lord hath
spoken. I have nourished and brought up children, and they have rebelled against me."

II. But, secondly, we have here brought before
us *the consequences of sin.* The first stage of iniquity is *riotous joy.* We must not keep that out
of view. There is a pleasure in it, *of a sort ;*
for if this were not so, men would not be found
indulging in it at all. There must be some kind
of exhilaration in the flowing bowl, or in the
wild thrill of sensual gratification, or in the gains
of dishonesty. In every sin there is something of
riot. "Stolen waters are sweet," perhaps, just
because they are stolen ; but the sweetness does

not last long. It turns to bitterness in the belly ; for, see, as the next result, *the waste which it occasions.* It wastes money, as we have to-day already remarked ; it wastes health ; it wears the body to decay ; but that is not the worst. These things here are set forth as but the outward indications of the waste of the soul. And, in truth, what a blasting thing sin is on the human spirit! How many who, in their youth, gave high promise of mental greatness, are now reduced to the merest drivellers, unable either to speak or write save under the influence of opium or alcohol! Ah! even as I speak, there rise up before me the fair forms of many noble fellows who, humanly speaking, might have counted on the highest positions in their several profession, but whose intellects have been weakened by their own enormities. Then, morally, how does sin blight the conscience, eating it out of the man, until he is ready for any iniquity! How it weakens the will, so that he who once stood firm as the oak against all storms, bends now like a reed before the most trifling breeze! Never will I forget how a wife, speaking once of the weakness of her husband's will before the fascination of drink and evil companions, said : " He used to be a firm and noble

fellow ; but he is a bairn noo." Yes, a child in
weakness ; but, alas ! alas ! very far indeed from
being a child in innocence. Sin had shorn the
locks of his strength ; and the Philistines, in the
shape of his own appetites, had bound him cap-
tive. Where has the father's portion gone in such
cases ? Where are the good gifts of God to the
soul now ? And who, in sinners like these, can
discern almost the faintest trace of the image of
God which once they bore ?

But observe, farther, as the next consequence,
we have *famine—i.e.*, spiritual want, and a craving after something that yet cannot be found.
There is nothing in iniquity that can give contentment to the spirit. " God has made us for
Himself, and our souls are restless till they rest
themselves in Him." We might illustrate this is
the history of sinners of every social position :
but, perhaps, you will be more convinced of the
truth on which I now insist if I give you a few
cases of men who had no external want unsatis-
fied, and yet were tormented by an aching void in
their hearts, craving for a happiness that would
not come at their desire ; and I gladly appropriate here the words of Dr. Hamilton, in his most
suggestive Lectures on the Book of Ecclesiastes :

—"We could call into court nearly as many witnesses as there have been hunters of happiness, mighty Nimrods in the chase of Pleasure, and Fame, and Favor. We might ask the statesman, and as we wished him a happy new year, Lord Dundas would answer: 'It had need to be a happier than the last, for I never knew one happy day in it.' We might ask the successful lawyer, and the wariest, luckiest, most self-complacent of them all would answer, as Lord Eldon was privately recording when the whole bar envied the Chancellor, 'A few weeks will send me to dear Encombe, as a short resting-place betwixt vexation and the grave.' We might ask the golden millionaire: 'You must be a happy man, Mr. Rothschild.' 'Happy! me happy! What! happy! when just as you are going to dine you have a letter placed in your hand, saying, "If you don't send me £500, I will blow your brains out!" Happy! when you have to sleep with pistols at your pillows.' We might ask the world-famed warrior, and get for answer the 'Miserere' of the Emperor-Monk (Charles V.,) or the sigh of a broken heart from St. Helena. We might ask the dazzling wit, and, faint with a glut of glory, yet disgusted with the creatures who

adored him Voltaire would condense the es-
sence of his existence into one word, '*ennui.*' And
we might ask the world's poet, and we would be
answered with an imprecation by that splendid
genius (Byron,) who

> ' Drank every cup of joy, heard every trump
> Of fame ; drank early, deeply drank ; drank draughts
> That common millions might have quenched, then died
> Of thirst, because there was no more to drink.' " *

But, descending from these cases, let us ask ourselves if, apart from God's favor, we have ever
had any real, solid, lasting joy? Let us analyze
our experiences in sin, and see if they have not
proved that there is no satisfaction in iniquity
but that, ever as we went on committing it, our
souls began to be in a greater and yet greater
want. Oh! shall we never become wise? Shall
we never learn that there is nothing but misery
while we are away from God? Ye who are seeking after happiness in earthly things, forbear.
Ye are pursuing a quest more visionary than
that of the child, who sets out to catch the pillars
of the many-colored rainbow in the far horizon.

---

* Hamilton's " Royal Preacher," pp. 26, 27.

Never, never can you obtain what you are seeking, save in God. Turn, then, and beseech Him to give you that which you desire. "Incline your ear, and come unto him : hear, and your soul shall live ; hearken diligently unto him, and then your soul shall delight itself in fatness ;" for, if the universal experience of humanity on this point were to be gathered into one expression, it would only indorse the words of Pollok :

> " Attempt how vain,
> With things of earthly sort, with aught but God,
> With aught but moral excellence, truth, and love,
> To satisfy and fill the immortal soul—
> To satisfy the ocean with a drop—
> To marry immortality to death,
> And with the unsubstantial shade of time
> To fill the embrace of all eternity."

Give over this mad endeavor, then. The cravings of your heart for happiness, if you only knew it, are inarticulate yearnings after God ; and the dissatisfaction and misery you feel in a life of sin, if you could but aright interpret them, are but the voice of your Father within you, saying evermore, " Come home to me ! Come home to me !" O let Him not call in vain ; but arise now and return to Him !

THE PRODIGAL SON,

II.

THE RESOLUTION.

" And when he came to himself, he said, How many hired servants of my father have bread enough and to spare, and I perish with hunger!

" I will arise and go to my father, and will say unto him, Father I have sinned against Heaven, and before thee,

" And am no more worthy to be called thy son : make me as one of thy hired servants.

" And he arose, and came to his father. But when he was yet a great way off, his father saw him, and had compassion, and ran, and fell on his neck, and kissed him."

LUKE xv., 17-20.

THE PRODIGAL SON.

II.

THE RESOLUTION.

We left the prodigal in the far land feeding swine, and longing to fill himself with the husks on which they fattened. To such a depth of degradation had he sunk, that he was willing to eat out of the same trough with the unclean animals which, as a Jew, he so abhorred. Yet, in this seeming "lowest deep," there was a "lower still," for even this poor luxury was denied him. "*No man gave unto him.*" The very swine were preferred to him, as belonging to a higher caste than he, and he was not allowed to share their fare. Ah, what a bitter humiliation was there in all this! He had left his home with many visions of prosperity and greatness beckoning him on, and

this was the result! Yet, bitter as it was, this
experience was the first thing that revealed him to
himself. As sometimes the drunken husband, reel-
ing home intoxicated, is sobered on the instant by
the sight of his dead wife, and has most vividly
recalled to him the day when, in the highest
hope and in the holiest affection, he had pledged
himself to love and cherish her ; so this setting
of the swine before him stung the prodigal into
a consciousness of his thorough desolation and
his terrible extremity. Till now he had kept on
hoping that " something would turn up " in his
favor, and enable him to retrieve his fortunes ; but
all such anticipations are henceforth gone. When
the hogs are set above him, it is all over with
him. He has nothing more to look for. Either
he must make up his mind to die of starvation,
or to go back to his father's house. This is
now his only alternative. Hitherto the choice
which he has set before him has always been between one or other of different ways of support-
ing himself in the far country ; but now the idea
of maintaining himself there is seen to be out
of the question, and, for the first time, he shapes
the alternative to himself thus—Will I remain
here, and die of starvation ? or will I go back to

the home which I so foolishly slighted in the
days of the past? Not all at once would he
decide upon his course. Even as he thought of
going back, difficulties would start up before him.
His consciousness of guilt would for a time un-
man him. Shame, too, would bid him stay.
Haply, also, the fear of being upbraided by his
father for the folly of his conduct would give
him pause. But, over and above these, there
was the strong, unanswerable, and importunate
argument of hunger. "At least, there is plenty
to eat at home," he thought; "and though I
may have to eat that plenty with bitter herbs, it
will be better than starvation here." So at
length, after a strong inward wrestle, the resolve
comes out, clear and strong—"I will arise, and
go to my father, and will say unto him, father, I
have sinned against heaven, and before thee, and
am no more worthy to be called thy son : make
me as one of thy hired servants." Plain, straight-
forward, humble, yet earnest, are the words
which he determines to take with him ; and that
nothing may intervene between the purpose and
the performance, he arose, just as he was, and set
out on his homeward way. The picture is perfect ; and in the history of many an outcast

whom treachery has first ruined, and then trampled under foot, it has been literally exempli-
fied ; nor do I know a kinder service we can do
to any poor prodigal whom the tide of our city
life may drift to our doors than just to put him
in the way of returning to his earthly father's
house; for, not unfrequently, that is only the
first step in the return of the erring one to God.
Perhaps such an one, led by the providence of
God, may have come casually into this house to-
day. Let me entreat him to go home, and glad-
den the hearts of those to whom he is dear.
By the memory of your mother's tenderness, and
your father's prayers; by the recollection of your
childhood's joys, and of your boyhood's happiness; by the obligation under which you feel
your parents laid you for your education, and
the opportunities of well-doing which you enjoyed—by all that is holiest and most treasured in the associations of the past, I implore
you to go home. And if words will not move
you, then let this touching scene impress your
heart. Behold that mother in her Highland
cottage, as she kneels at evening prayer. Draw
near and listen to the words she utters, as the
big tears course down her cheeks : " *Lord*," she

says, "*have mercy on that poor lassie, wherever she may be this night. Let her not die in her sins. But bring her back to me again, that I may bring her back to Thee.*" She rises from her knees, goes out to look through the darkness if, perchance, the wanderer may be near. She comes in and shuts the door, but leaves it unbarred, saying the while—"*I will not bolt it, lest she should come when I'm asleep, and I would not like her to find my door locked against her.*" Oh, is there nothing in all this to impel you homeward? Go back! go back! the door into a true parent's heart, like that of the home of which I have spoken, *is usually on the latch to an erring child*, and the truest joy you have known for many a day will be when you weep out your penitence in your father's arms.

But we must not forget that this is not merely a literal history. It is a parable, having a spiritual meaning. The prodigal, as we saw in the last discourse, represents the sinner—and the scene depicted in the verses now before us describes what we may call the crisis of conversion. Now, thus regarded, the language is most suggestive, and illustrates these important things, namely, the sinner's true condition so long as he is away from God, the means by which this condition is changed, the reflections made by him after this change, and the resolution to which his reflections lead.

I. In the first place, we have brought before us *the true condition of the sinner so long as he is away from God.* "When he came to himself :" that implies that in some very real sense he had not been perfectly himself. Generally, commentators have supposed that the reference here is to insanity, and they tell us, with perfect truth, that the sinner is, in some respects, like a madman. He follows delusions as if they were realities, and he treats realities as if they were delusions. His moral nature is perverted, just as the lunatic's intellect is beclouded ; and, in regard to duty, he makes mistakes similar to those which the maniac makes in ordinary matters. So he may well be styled mad ; but there is this solemn difference between him and the ordinary lunatic, that while insanity cancels responsibility, the sinner is not only blameworthy for his moral perversity, but his responsibility continues in spite of it. Although, however, there are thus many interesting and striking points of resemblance be-

tween the condition of the maniac and that of the
sinner, I am not sure that the "coming to himself," in the verse before me, suggests the being
"beside himself," as the condition out of which
he came. Equally it may imply that he was "beneath himself," or that there was in him a certain unconsciousness, out of which he required to
be roused before he could be thoroughly himself.
When, for example, one has fainted away and re-
covers, we say that "he has come to himself
again," implying that his consciousness has returned. Now, in my view, this is the preferable
way of looking at the analogy of my text. The
moral nature of this poor youth was virtually
dead. His conscience had become seared, so
that he was, in a manner, unconscious that there
was such a faculty within him. It was there, but
it was asleep. It was there, but it was so precisely as the intellectual nature is in a man when
he is in a faint: it was inoperative, it was not
consciously possessed by him. At length, however, roused by a sense of his degradation,
and the touch of God's Spirit, it awoke, and
then he came to himself. The sinner's higher
nature is dormant in him. He has a spiritual
faculty which allies him with God, and which,

as the noblest part of his nature, is most really
and truly himself. But he is not conscious
that he has it. It is dead within him. He has
overlaid it with trespasses and sins. Hence he is
not himself. I do not mean, of course, that his
personal identity is gone, but rather that the noblest part of his nature has been as good as lost
by him. The spiritual, as distinguished from the
mere intellectual, has become virtually non-existent. His animal nature may be as strong as ever.
His intellect may be brilliant and acute. Even in
regard to morals he may be irreproachable by his
fellow-men ; but in that part of his being that
allies him with God he never dwells. He lives, so
to say, on the ground-floor of the soul-house, on
earth and among earthly things. His appetites,
passions, and desires are strong ; his intellect even
may be vigorous and clear ; but it is only exer-
cised regarding natural things. He does not
know those things which can be only " spiritually
discerned." His soul has no outlook toward heaven, and that part of his nature which was intended to be its crowning glory, and which allies
him to heaven, is shut up and tenantless, like a
dusty attic. He is not himself.

II. But we have here, secondly, *the change of this condition :* "he came to himself." A new light broke upon this youth in the midst of his darkness. He saw things as he had never before perceived them. Not till now did he discover the guilt and issue of the course which he had been pursuing ; and never in his past experience had his father's house seemed to him precious. For the first time since he left his home, he awoke from " the dream his life-long fever gave him," and things as they were stood unveiled before him. Now, so it is with the sinner. His conversion, too, is in its first stage an awakening. New thoughts stir within his soul ; new feelings vibrate in his bosom. He begins to see what before had been to him almost as a landscape is to a man born blind. It is not that new things are called into existence outside of him, for all things are there as they were before. It is rather that his eyes have been opened to see them ; and the wonder of his whole subsequent life is, that he never saw them until then. He perceives now the danger in which he stands; and recognizing the ability and willingness of God to help him, he cries, like Peter, weltering in the waters, " Lord, save me ; I perish." Such being the change which is here called a coming to himself, the question presents itself, How is this alteration brought about in the sinner? The answer is important, and though it will take us into the deep things of spiritual experience, I shall endeavor to put it clearly and distinctly before you.

Let me ask you to recall what I have already said regarding the relation of the three parables in this chapter to each other. The first two set before us God seeking and finding the sinner, through the incarnation of the Son, and the agency of the Spirit. The third shows us the sinner seeking God. But we are not to suppose that these are separate pictures of distinct conversions. On the contrary, they are all three true of every real conversion. Viewed from the divine side, God seeks the sinner ; but we, who see only the earthly side, perceive only the sinner rising and returning to God. It did not lie in the Saviour's way in this story to illustrate either the connection of His own sacrificial work, or that of the Spirit's agency, with conversion. Indeed, the introduction of anything like a representation of either of these would only have marred the unity of the parable. But in dealing with conversion, we have

to remember that there is a divine side to the subject as well as a human one, and that the full
truth regarding it is to be had, not by taking each
side separately, but by combining both. Thus it
is a fact that, from first to last in a sinner's conversion, there is and must be the special agency
of the Divine Spirit; but it is also a fact that
there is in it a human activity. The Spirit works;
but then He does so in harmony with the constitution of the human soul, and in such a way that
the soul is not conscious of His operations as
anything distinct from the workings of its own
faculties. The Spirit goes before the truth to
prepare its way, by providences and other means
at His disposal. The Spirit comes with the truth
to give it power. This He does in a manner
which He has not been pleased anywhere to explain. But still it is in connection with the truth
that He operates; and His operations are not of ·
such a nature that the soul can identify them at
the time as His, and as apart from the workings
of its own powers. To the eye of a spiritual being, God's agency is conspicuous from the begin-
ning, and the whole work may be called His. To
the eye of a man, the sinner alone is visible, and
the whole thing may be said to be done by him-

self. The full truth is, that the man is working out his own salvation, because God is working in him to will and to do of His good pleasure. Or, as Jonathan Edwards has expressed it, the whole thing is brought about by " *God's working all, and man's acting all.*" Yet, even in reference to God's working, let us remember that He employs always appropriate means. The great end He has in view is to awaken the soul to spiritual things, to get it to perceive its danger, and to apprehend the means of salvation which He has provided. Now, by the dispensations of His providence, He may dispose the soul to receive the truth on these subjects in many ways. Affliction is one of the most common,—disease, as it were, ringing the alarm-bell of the soul, and rousing it to face eternal realities. Thus it was with Chalmers, and many more, in whom the crisis of being has been as signally marked. Sometimes, again, He uses the early associations of home, and through means of them procures the opening of the heart, which had remained shut even against the presence of severest affliction. Thus it was with the poor sailor lying in the hospital of one of our seaports, who remained unmoved by every appeal addressed to him, until the missionary, perceiving that he was a Scotsman, sat down beside his bed and sang, to the fine old tune of Coleshill, the Psalmist's words, as rendered in the metrical version used in the churches and homes of his native land :

> Such pity as a father hath
> Unto his children dear,
> Like pity shows the Lord to such
> As worship Him in fear.

When he heard the old familiar strain, he started up at once, and said, " Who taught *you* that ? I.haven't heard it since I heard my father sing it at family worship." So, the truth having found an entrance through the portals of memory, the missionary was not long in leading him to Christ. Occasionally, again, the heart is opened, and the man awakened, through the means of natural affection. Thus it was with him of whom John Ashworth tells, who left his breakfast-table one Sabbath morning for a few minutes to arrange with some comrades about going out dog-fighting in the forenoon. When he returned, he saw tears standing in the eyes of his little daughter, as she sat finishing her meal, and ready dressed for Sunday school. " What ails thee ?" said he, as he kindly looked at her. " I don't want you to go with these bad men," she answered. "It is the Lord's day, and God will be sure to see you." "Bless the child," said he ; "how she talks! Never mind me, dear, but go to school." Still, however, she sat in sorrow, and as the tears flowed thickly down her cheeks, she said again, "Don't go, father." "Well, then," said he, "I won't go. So go to the school with thee, and be happy." And he did not go, but in the evening went with her to public worship ; and she found for him the places, for she was the better scholar of the two. And by and by, as the result of all this, he came to himself, and went to his Father, and is now an honored and useful member of the Christian Church. Nay, sometimes even the ribald profanity of the wicked man has been the means employed by God to rouse him to his higher self. During the days of Whitefield and his coadjutors, Mr. Thorpe, and several like-minded companions in Yorkshire, undertook to mimic and travesty the preaching of these great Evangelists. One after another, they mounted a table, and set themselves to caricature one or other of God's servants. Mr. Thorpe's turn came last, and, in the regardlessness of his spirit, as he ascended the table, he said, "I shall beat you all." The Bible

was handed to him. It opened—how, he knew
not, but those who saw God's side of the affair,
would perceive His hand open it—at Luke xiii., 3,
"Except ye repent, ye shall all likewise perish."
The moment he read, his soul was impressed. He
saw clearly the nature and importance of the subject; and he afterwards said, if he ever preached
with the assistance of the Holy Spirit, it was at
that time. When he had finished—levelled, as it
were, by the recoil of the gun which he had
thought to fire at God's servants—he retired to
weep over his sins, and became in the end an
able and useful minister of the New Testament.
Or, not to multiply instances, God may use the
ordinary means of curiosity and the preaching
of the truth to lead up to this awakening. So
it was with one of whom I have been told, who
was of excellent moral character, a zealous ad-
vocate of total abstinence, and a most intellectual man, but, unhappily, also an unbeliever.
Passing along the street one Lord's-day morning, he came to the door of a church where a
minister preached who was well known for his
labors in the temperance cause, and he said
within himself, "I have heard of this man; I
should like to go in." But he had not been

within a house of God for ten years, and he felt ashamed to venture. He went away fully a quarter of a mile past the church, but still he felt as if he must go back. So he returned and entered the sanctuary. In the course of the sermon, something was said which stirred him to the very depths. His knees smote against each other. He sat trembling and astonished. He came again. He heard a Bible-class announced for a certain evening. He went to that. He became interested in the inquiries which were there prosecuted; and at length, coming fully to himself, he went to his Father, writing to the minister whom God had used all through in these words :—" With the long and dreary winter that has passed away has gone the winter of my unbelief; and while I attribute this result to a higher than human power, permit me to say that you have been the channel through which that power was conveyed, first from the pulpit, and afterwards by your kind and generous sympathy, for which I hope I shall ever be truly grateful." Now, I have brought out these cases to show you how in conversion, all, from the human side, is perfectly natural, while from the divine all is of God. The doc-

trine of the special agency of the Spirit in conversion, thus viewed, is a parallel instance to
that of the great doctrine of the special providence of God. It might, indeed, almost be described as special providence working in the department of spiritual things; and God's agency
and man's agency are united in conversion, just
as they are united in the actions of every day.
We cannot be saved without the Spirit's agency;
but neither, again, can the Spirit save us except
through our own activity in believing.and obeying the truth. The Spirit's agency is necessary
to faith and repentance, but it is the sinner that
believes and repents. It is impossible to say
where the one agency terminates, and the other
begins. Rather, as it seems to me, do they mu-
tually interpenetrate each other, only, as these parables make plain, God's seeking always precedes
the sinner's rising.

III. But it is time now that we should consider *the prodigal's reflections on coming to himself.*
They were twofold—having regard, first, to himself, and, second, to his father's house.

In reference to himself, he said—"I perish
with hunger." Now, as I have already hinted,

there was distinct progress here. Never before had this youth allowed himself to think that death by starvation was to be the issue if he remained in the far land; but so soon as that clearly shaped itself to him, he took his resolution to arise. It is the same with men, and their return to God. I believe if we could narrow down the choice of the sinner to one or other of these two alternatives—everlasting destruction as the consequence of guilt, or eternal salvation, through faith in Jesus Christ—we should have no difficulty in impelling him to decide in the right direction; but because he persists in believing that there is some loophole left him, through which he may escape, even if he should not accept salvation through Christ, he continues indifferent to the statements of the gospel. I do not think that there are many men who believe that they are going to everlasting perdition. There are, indeed, multitudes of deplorably wicked persons; yet I cannot think that they ever really consider that they are on the way to hell. They have the feeling that things are not just so bad with them as that yet; they fancy that, somehow or other, they hardly know how, in spite of all that they are, and all that they have done, they shall still escape ; and so they go thoughtlessly on. They imagine that God will not, as they say, " be strict to mark iniquity with them ;" or they think that sin cannot be such a dreadful thing after all ; or they flatter themselves that they will, at some future period, take thought and repent; and they say, meanwhile, " There's time enough yet." Thus each one has his own vague hope that, after all, "he shall not surely die." So it is that Satan keeps continually repeating the old lie wherewith he deluded our common parents to their ruin. But when the sinner comes to himself, all these deceptions are swept away. He sees only the fearful fact, " ' I perish.' Away from God, I must be, I cannot but be, eternally destroyed ;" and this, taken together with his belief in God's offer of salvation, stirs him up to arise and to return to his Father. Awake, O sinner! to the danger in which you stand. If you continue as you are, there is nothing but destruction before you. If you neglect the great salvation, there is no possibility of escape for you. Between two such alternatives, who would hesitate as to his choice ?

But the prodigal's reflections had reference

also to his father's house. He said—" How
many hired servants of my father's have bread
enough and to spare !" Bread !—once he thought
of greatness and wealth ;—now, however, he will
be content with bread—yea, if he could only have
what many a time he had seen his father's servants lay aside as not required by them, he would
be content. There was enough at home, if he
were only there. Now, similarly, the sinner, in
conversion, comes to the persuasion that there is
plenty for him in God. If you ask how this is
brought about in him, I answer, by his belief of
the statements of the gospel ; for it is here that
we must bring in the doctrine of the Cross. It
is possible for one to be aroused to a sense of
his danger, and yet go no further. Many have
been " awakened," as the phrase is, without being
converted. They have had a glimpse of the
awful truth, that they were perishing ; but they
have not believed the good news of salvation in
Jesus, and so they have continued in their sins.
They found that they were in want, but they did
not seem to know that there was bread in their
Father's house. In every real conversation, however, we have both things believed ; and the belief of both is connected with the Cross of Christ,

for there the sinner learns both how fearful a thing sin is, and how full of love to him God is. He sees, in Christ's death, an atonement for sin of infinite value, and unlimited sufficiency. There is enough in it to meet his need—yea, *enough and to spare ;* salvation, not for him alone, but for all who choose to avail themselves of it; and the belief of that, coupled with his appalling sense of present danger and the necessity, impels him to resolve. Let the sinner take note of this, that he may be encouraged, not to go on in sin, but " to repent and be converted." There is hope for ·him. " Christ Jesus is the propitiation for the sins of the whole world. " He is able to save unto the uttermost all that cometh unto God.by Him, seeing he ever liveth to make intercession for them." Who would starve with such plenty at hand? who would die eternally with such life put in his offer? There is no stint in the provision which God has made for us in the gospel feast. There is enough and to spare. Enough for all the guests, and yet abundance besides. "Yet there is room"—room in the love of God's heart; room in the sufficiency of the work of Christ; room in the Church below; room in the sanctuary above; room for sin-

ners of every age and degree, and color and
clime ;—yea, room, O starving one! for thee, if
only thou wilt take thy place at the board, and
put on the wedding garment which thy Lord has
furnished.

IV. I dare not conclude without noticing, however briefly, *the resolution to which those reflections
led.* "I will arise and go to my father, and will
say unto him, Father, I have sinned against
heaven and before thee, and am no more worthy
to be called thy son. Make me as one of thy
hired servants." This youth determined, there
and then, to go back to his home; not, however,
in a dogged, sullen, defiant spirit, but in a thoroughly penitent disposition. He blames no one
but himself; he resolves to make a full and frank
acknowledgment of his folly; and, instead of
claiming anything as a rightful portion, he is willing to be treated as a servant. Now, taking
this as representing the sinner's repentance, one
or two things need to be noted, as suggested
by it.

In the first place, there is an unreserved confession of sin : "*Father, I have sinned against
heaven and before thee.*" He does not soften

matters, and speak of his "faults" or his "failings." He does not say, in a self-extenuating way, "I have been a little wild;" but he puts the plain truth forth in all its hideousness, "I have *sinned!*" Neither, again, does he cast the blame on others. He does not say, "So-and-so led me astray;" "If it had not been for the companions by whom I was surrounded, I had never come to this;" or, "If I had only been in other circumstances, I would have kept myself from iniquity." No; his language is, "*I* have sinned; the guilt is mine. I have no wish to evade it, or explain it away. I am ashamed of myself."

Yet, once more, the enormity of his wickedness before heaven is that which most distresses him. He had brought many evils on himself. He had inflicted great injuries upon others ; but that which most burdens him now is, that he has sinned against God—the *Father* who has done so much for him, and has even, after all, and, above all, sent His Son into the world to make atonement for his guilt. This is painful to him in the extreme, and he can do nothing but weep over it; but his tears, in the estimation of God, are of more value than the glittering diamond, for they tell Him that He has found at last His long-lost child, not simply in the outward form that stands before him, but also in the heart out of which this sorrow comes. This is true penitence. This is the broken spirit, exhaling an odor sweeter far than that which came from the alabaster vase of spikenard in Mary's hand. This is the contrite heart which the Lord will not despise.

But, looking again at the resolution before us, we find in it a determination to personal exertion : " *I will arise !*" The prodigal did not wait till some one else should come and lift him, and carry him to his home. He was fully persuaded that if ever he reached his father's house, it could only be by travelling the distance for himself : so he arose and went. Now, similarly with the sinner, though the distance between him and God is not physical, but moral, yet, if he would be saved, there must be the putting forth of his own individual human agency. He does not require to rise from the spot where he is, and go away to some far distant country, in order to return to God. He may pass through the whole transition while yet he is in one and the same earthly spot. The coming is spiritual. It is the

restoring of his heart to God : the giving back of
his love, and loyalty, and allegiance to his Heavenly Father : the surrender to God of the sovereignty of his soul which, in the outset of his career, he had determined to retain to himself.
Now, this restoration of the soul to God, this giving back of itself to the Father, is the soul's own
act ; and in this self-submission to Jehovah—this
rendering back of itself by the soul to God, as
its proper possessor—we have the consummation
of conversion. No doubt, as I have said, the
Spirit is in it all ; yet the soul *gives itself up*, and
we must be on our guard against delaying this
self-renunciation on the plea of *waiting for the
Spirit*. To put off, on this ground, would be
just as foolish in us as it would have been in the
prodigal here to have said—" I will wait till
some one lifts me up, and carries me home."
Multitudes, however, think of the Spirit's agency
as of some influence which, distinct from, and
external to, themselves, is to take them, and,
apart from any action of their own, carry them
into salvation. But this is an utter delusion.
The Spirit works for us by working in us, and
through us ; and His agency is not such as we
can distinguish, apart from the common opera-

tion of our faculties. Hence, if we wish the Spirit to lead us to give back our souls to God, we must ourselves seek to make this spiritual surrender ; and when we do, we shall discover that He has been beforehand with us, and has already anticipated us with His quickening grace.

Finally, here, this resolution was promptly acted upon : "*He arose and went to his father.*" Just as he was, all tattered and filthy, he went back. He did not say, looking at his garments the while, "I cannot go in this plight ; I must wash myself, and change my raiment, and then set out." Had he mused in that fashion, he would probably never have returned ; but he went as he was. So, in conversion, the sinner gives himself back to God just as he is. He does not seek to make himself better. He delays not to work out for himself a robe of righteousness. He waits not even for deeper feelings, or for more intense conviction. He puts himself into God's hands, sure that, for Christ's sake, He will make him all that he should be. "Such as I am," he says, "take me and make me such as Thou wouldst have me to be." This is the whole matter. This *only !* but *all* this ; and if there be any one here to-day moved by the presentation of these truths, let me beseech him now, where he is, and as he is, to give himself back to the Father, without reservation and without delay.

> " Just as thou art, without one trace
> Of love, or joy, or inward grace,
> Or meetness for the heavenly place,
> O guilty sinner, come !"

" Ho, every one that thirsteth, come ye to the waters, and he that hath no money ; come ye, buy wine and milk without money and without price. Wherefore do ye spend money for that which is not bread ? and your labor for that which satisfieth not ? hearken diligently unto me, and let your soul delight itself in fatness. Incline your ear, and come unto me : hear, and your soul shall live ; and I will make an everlasting covenant with you, even the sure mercies of David." " Come unto me, all ye that labor and are heavy laden, and I will give you rest." " The Spirit and the bride say, Come ; and let him that heareth say, Come. And let him that is athirst come. And whosoever will, let him take the water of life freely." Spirit of the Living God ! let some soul to-day hear this heavenly home-call, and return to Thee.

THE PRODIGAL SON.

III.

THE RETURN.

" And he arose, and came to his father. But when he was yet a great way off, his father saw him, and had compassion, and ran, and fell on his neck, and kissed him.

" And the son said unto him, Father, I have sinned against Heaven, and in thy sight, and am no more worthy to be called thy son.

" But the father said to his servants, Bring forth the best robe, and put it on him ; and put a ring on his hand, and shoes on his feet :

" And bring hither the fatted calf, and kill it ; and let us eat, and be merry :

" For this my son was dead, and is alive again ; he was lost, and is found. And they began to be merry."

LUKE, xv., 20-24.

THE PRODIGAL SON.

III.

THE RETURN.

MANY years have passed since the prodigal's departure from his father's house, but all things there have continued outwardly as they were. The same air of prosperity is about the place. In spring-time the carol of the plough-boy, and in harvest the song of the reaper, have been heard as before. If anything, the old people have grown more venerable in aspect; their gait has become more stooping, and their movements are slower; while the wrinkles on their foreheads have deepened, and grey hairs are here and there among their locks; but the same neat attention to appearance characterizes them both, and a calm contentment sits upon their faces.

Their son has conducted himself with decorum, and by his energy and care has relieved his father from all anxiety as to worldly things ; and their servants have been so long beneath their roof, that they have come to regard themselves, and to be regarded by others, as members of the family. To the casual visitor everything would seem delightful, and many might have envied the gladness that appeared to dwell among them. But external things are no sure indication of that which lies beneath them ; for, even in this home, there is a *skeleton*. A sorrow, all the heavier that it is never spoken, lies upon the parents' hearts, revealed only by the long-fixed, abstracted gaze that comes occasionally across their countenances, or by the heavy, deep-drawn sigh, which, in thoughtful moments, one or other heaves. No ingenious questioning of yours will evoke their confidence, or draw from them a description of their cross ; but, when you go, at eventide, to the servants' hall, you may hear the elder among them whispering to the younger something about master's "other" son ; and when you ask them what they mean, they will tell you how, long ago, there was a younger son in the family—the idol of them all. They will never weary of praising his frank open-heartedness, so different from the stiff preciseness of his brother; they will rehearse to you the jokes he made, and the songs he used to sing, and the kind things he did to all about him. They will relate, mayhap, how, when one of them was seized with sudden and dangerous illness, it was he who rode through the pelting rain to hasten for the medical man; it was he who sat up through the dreary night-hours, seeking to soothe the sufferer; it was he who was always ready with his help and his hand—the darling of the family, the pride of the country-side. Then, with the gathering tear in the eye, they will tell how something took him, they never found out precisely what; and he left the house and went away, no one knew whither, and had never been heard of since. Then they will assure you that for all so quiet and calm as he looked, " master " had never been the same since he had gone, but went about the house, seeming to have lost a part of himself; and that even yet, day after day, he would go to the hill-top yonder, and look this way and that way, as if he were expecting him to come again; but that he never named his name, and they only knew how keen were his feelings in the matter from one constant petition in his family prayer—"That God might bring the wanderer home."

Ah! how many houses in the land have just such a skeleton within as this! Would God that in each case the issue were as it was here! For, lo! rounding the corner of the lane, the long-lost son is seen "afar off." Many a weary foot he has travelled, sustained by the prospect of reaching home at last; yet when at length the old familiar place comes first into his view, strange misgivings fill his heart. Hope spurred him on till then, but now fears begin to work. "Will my father receive me after all?" "How can I face him in this pitiful plight?" "Would it not be better to go back?" These and kindred questionings arise within him, and he lingers in timid irresolution. But before he is aware, his faltering feelings are banished in a way at once the most unexpected and the most effectual. For his father had been, as his custom was, upon the outlook for him; and though his raiment was ragged, and his face haggard, and his whole appearance changed, there was still that about him, in walk, or shape, or feature, by which at once the old man recognized him. And he ran and embraced him, and kissed him. There were no words spoken on his side ; for, when the heart is fullest, it can speak only through tears. Like Jacob with Joseph, " he fell on his neck, and wept a good while." No taunt about the past was uttered ; no gibe escaped him about the present appearance of his son. It was enough that it was he come home again ; and he would take him, not to his house merely, but to his heart. In that embrace the prodigal's misgivings melted all away. There was no question now about his reception. He had been already welcomed ; and so with a deeper feeling than he had known when he made the resolution to employ them, he repeated the words, " *Father, I have sinned against heaven and in thy sight, and am no more worthy to be called thy son*," but he did not add, " Make me as one of thy hired servants." That, he felt, would have been to insult the generous affection of his father, who had already taken him back into the old place of son ; so, gladly and gratefully, he accepts the kindness, and goes forward with him to the dwelling. When they reached the house, the order was given by the father to the servants, " Bring forth the best robe and put it on him ; and put a ring on his hand, and shoes on his feet ; and bring hither the fatted calf, and let us eat and be merry ;" while, that all may know the reason of this unwonted joy, the proclamation was made, "For this my son was dead, and is alive again : he was lost, and is found."

Not always thus, however, are returning children received by earthly parents ; and before I pass to the spiritual meaning of this portion of the parable, permit me to point from it a moral for the guidance of those who are heads of families among us. We who are in that position have two opposite dangers to avoid. On the one hand, we have to watch against that laxity of discipline which permits children to do just as they please ; and, on the other, we have to keep from that stern and unrelenting severity which visits every fault with rigid punishment, and presents a cold, unfeeling aspect to the child. It is hard to say which of these two evils is the more pernicious ; but, in general, we are prone to fall into the former when our children are very young ; and, into the latter when they grow older, and verge toward manhood and womanhood. Now it is especially the extreme of sternness which is reproved by the conduct of the father here described. We ought to recognize the birth of individuality in our children ; and, as they advance in years, we ought to feel that we are to rule them through the intellect and the affections, and not by the force of mere authority. There is a parental intolerance which is as harsh and overbearing, and to the full as disastrous, as any infringement of civil or religious liberty by a government can ever be. And, in our desire to rule as the family governors, we ought never to forget the kind of rule which we are to exercise. I willingly admit that, even in the case of grown-up sons and daughters, there may be offences committed which require that we should show displeasure ; but we should beware of *so* showing it, as to drive them from our homes at the very time when most they need to feel the influence of our love, and to be regulated by the force of our example. I have heard of a minister of the gospel turning one of his sons out of doors for nothing worse than such pranks as lads, in the exuberance of their spirits, are prone to indulge in. The mother went with him for a portion of his way, and talked and prayed with him as only a mother can ; and, in his case, the issue was that he rose to a position of honor, not only in the nation, but in the Church. Still, if it had been otherwise, and the youth had gone to ruin, would not his father have been chargeable in some degree with the murder of his soul? The skillful angler, when he hooks a noble fish, is never too anxious to bring it to the shore. *He gives it line,* and lets it run awhile, until at length, weary with its splashing, it becomes an easy prey. So in fishing for men, and especially for our own children, we must not make the cord too tight, lest it break, and they go far from us; but with a holy guile, and with a loving tenderness, while we still keep hold of them, we must *give them line*, only thereby in the end to bring them more securely to the Lord. So again, when a son or a daughter has gone astray, and comes back to us, we should act as this father did. We should not upbraid, or sneer, or ridicule, or condemn. We may be sure that there has been enough of bitterness in the conscience of the offender, before the mind was made up to come to us again. The heart and the home should be opened as before, and nothing should come from us that would painfully remind the prodigal of past iniquity. How deeply some men have sinned at once against their own better nature and against God, by adopting an opposite course! I have been told of a father coming into a house where, unknown to him, his daughter was at the moment a guest ; and, though her heart was yearning for a kindly word from him, there was nothing but a cold, silent greeting accorded to her. Why ? because she had given her heart and her hand to a good man, whose only fault, even in her father's eyes, was that he was poor. What an idea that man must have of God, if this be his notion of fatherhood ! and what a dread that shrinking one must have of Jehovah, if her earthly father is to be to her a type of the Father in Heaven ! A few years ago it was stated in the English newspapers that a Bishop, who had died possessed of thousands, had deliberately declined to leave a portion to a daughter, simply on the ground that she had married, against his will, a poor clergyman of the very Church of which he was a dignitary ! Nor was he content with that ; but in his will, and with his own account in view, he actually vindicated his conduct on the score of justice and of duty. Alas for us, if God had thus inexorably cut us off from all hope of inheritance ! Since, then, such paltry grounds as these are, in some cases, sufficient to create implacable resentment in a parent's heart, we need not be surprised to find that frequently, when sin has been commit-

ted, the father's house is shut against the offender. " *He shall never darken my door again ;*" or,
" *I will have nothing more to do with her, she has made
her own bed, and must lie upon it.*" These are
expressions, alas ! which are sometimes heard
from those who have what they call " ill-doing "
children. But do they ever think how much the
knowledge that they are thus unrelenting does to
drive the poor wanderer into more terrible iniquity ? or how, perhaps, their cruel harshness
may even keep the prodigal from turning to God ?
—as he says, " If my father will not hearken
to me, how can I hope that God will forgive
me ?" Oh ! let us remember that " WE ARE
SAVED BY HOPE," not by fear. You may bring
your child back to rectitude by giving him
ground to hope for something from your affection ; you will never reform him by making him
afraid of you. The matron of a female educa-
tional hospital in Edinburgh told me, recently, a
most interesting history. One of her scholars,
after she had left the hospital, fell into evil
courses, and became openly abandoned ; hearing
of her case, my friend tracked her from one den
of infamy to another, braving dangers which, for
a Christian lady, are more terrible than the dead-

liest charge is to a soldier. At length she found her ; and, after long dealing with her, in which she was aided by a devoted minister of Christ, and blessed, as she believes, by the Holy Spirit, she succeeded in taking her to her mother's house, in a quiet rural retreat. Now, just suppose, for a moment, that after all the exertions of these friends, the mother had said, " *No, she shall not come here. I will not have my household polluted by her presence.*" What would have been the effect upon the girl ? Would it not have sent her back again to sin ? and would not she, from whom she had the greatest reason to expect affection, have been, in that case, the cause of her ultimate ruin ? As it was, however, the mother, like the father here, " *kissed the past into forgetfulness,*" and, without upbraiding of any sort, took her to her home once more. Thus it should always be ; for if we would hold our children back from sin, or bring them again from the evil ways into which they may have fallen, we must bind them by the spell, and draw them by the magnetism of love. Let us make home attractive by the sweet influences of affection ; so shall we best preserve our young people from going astray ; and, when they have fallen, let us be

sure that only tenderness and affection will ever
lift them up again.

> "Forget not thou hast often sinned,
> And sinful yet must be ;
> Deal gently with the erring one,
> As thy God hath dealt with thee."

It is time, however, that we should look at the
spiritual meaning of this portion of the parable ;
and here the question presents itself, What are
we to understand by the reception given by the
father to the returning prodigal? The answer
may be given in a single sentence,—It is the
welcome given to the repentant sinner by God
the Father. But while this is the true principle
of interpretation, some things must be added at
once to prevent misconception, and to bring out
more vividly the truths which are intended to be
symbolized by the incidents here recorded.

And, in the first place, when we read of the
prodigal being *a great way off*, and so are led to
think of his return as a long and toilsome journey,
we are not to suppose that conversion is neces-
sarily a protracted process. The coming back, of
course, in the parable must correspond to the
departure into the far land ; and though frequently

there is a considerable time of anxiety and strug-
gle between the moment of awakening and the
time when the soul finds joy and peace in believing, yet this dark middle-passage is by no means
essential. Rather it is the result either of faulty
views as to the way of salvation, or of a want of
faith in the truth as it is presented to the sinner.
There was no such long interval between conviction and conversion in the case of those who were
born again on the day of Pentecost, or in that of
Saul of Tarsus, or in that of the Philippian jailer;
and I cannot but think that, unintentionally of
course, much harm has been done in this matter
by the records of some Christian biographies, and
even by such an admirable allegory as "The
Pilgrim's Progress." No doubt the representations given are true to actual experience in many
instances ; but all such experiences spring from an
unwillingness on the part of individuals to submit
themselves at once to the righteousness of God,
and perhaps, also, from an imperfect understanding by them of the real nature of the gospel. We
ought not, therefore, to imagine that such cases
are normal instances, and that every conversion
to be genuine must be in every respect like them.
The distance at which the sinner stands from

God is spiritual, not material; and whensoever the soul gives itself up to Jehovah to be saved, in His way, through Jesus Christ, that is the moment of conversion. It may be long, in many cases it has been long, after moral thoughtfulness and spiritual anxiety have been produced, before the individual comes to this unreserved submission. But it need not be long, and it should not be long. Nay, it would not be long if the gospel, in its freeness and fullness, were by the soul clearly understood and thoroughly believed. The way is prolonged by the fact that the sinner either does not know, or will not believe the glad tidings of salvation through the crucified Redeemer. On this point I cannot refrain from reproducing an anecdote which I heard one evening in conversation from the lips of Mr. Spurgeon. An earnest young evangelist on his way one morning from Granton to Edinburgh, overtook a Newhaven fishwife carrying her basket to the market. Anxious to do some good, he said to her, " There you go with your burden on your back. Once I had a heavier load than that, but, thank God, I have got rid of it now." "Oh," she replied, "you mean the burden that John Bunyan speaks of; I know all about that;

but I have got rid of mine many and many a
year ago." "I am happy to hear of it," said
the evangelist. "Yes," she answered ; "but do
you know I don't think that man Evangelist was
a right preacher of the gospel at all. When
Christian asked him where he was to go, he said,
Do you see yonder wicket-gate? He said he
didn't, and it was no wonder. He asked again,
Do you see yonder shining light? and he said he
did ; and then Evangelist directed him to make
for that. Now, what business had he to speak
either about the shining light or the wicket-
gate? Couldn't he have pointed him at once to
the Redeemer's cross? Christian never did lose
his burden till he saw that cross ; and he
might have seen it sooner if Evangelist had
known his business better. Much good he got,
too, by making for the shining light! Why, before he knew where he was, he was floundering
in the Slough of Despond ; and if it had not
been for the man Help, he would never have got
out." " What !" said the evangelist to her, " were
you never in the Slough of Despond?" "Ay,
many a time, many a time," was the reply ;
"but let me tell you, young man, it's a hantel
easier to get through that slough with your

burden off, than with your burden on!" Now, though as a record of what often actually happens, and of what really occurred in his own history, the immortal allegorist has given us a truthful portraiture, the Christian fishwife was in the right; for the moment a sinner rightly apprehends and thoroughly believes the doctrine of the cross, he loses his sin-burden; and this may be after no painfully protracted process of agony and inward conflict. In point of fact, awakening conversion, and peace may be all but simultaneous, and the soul may come to a full knowledge of its guilt almost at the same moment that it embraces the Saviour whom God has provided. Understand, therefore, it is not needed that you go through a long series of terrible experiences, called by some old divines "*law-work;*" but you may, where you are and as you are, enter into peace by simply accepting deliverance through the crucified Redeemer.

Again, when we read that the father saw his son " a great way off, and had compassion on him, and ran and fell on his neck and kissed him," we are not to imagine that God at such a time comes to the sinner in any special and peculiar manner other than that set before us in the gospel. Admirably has one said here—"The coming out of the father to meet his son. figuratively exhibits the sending of the Son." * All the way to the Cross of Calvary has God come, running to meet sinners. What a long way that is, who can tell? for who can measure the distance from the throne of glory to the dust of death? That cross is the meeting-place between the righteous God and the repentant prodigal. In Christ God has come in infinite compassion, showing how He can be a just God and a Saviour ; and when we grasp that cross in simple faith, it is then that He embraces us and takes us home to his heart. "In Christ," the Father has come as far as He righteously can come to save sinners ; and when the sinner is by faith "in Christ" also, then is he received by God. Hence the action of the Father, as portrayed in this parable, is only a pictorial representation of the truth Paul proclaims as the ministry of reconciliation, to wit, that "God was in Christ, reconciling the world unto Himself, not imputing their trespasses unto them ;" and

---

* Von Gerlach, quoted by Stier in his commentary on this passage.

concerning which he says, " Now, then, we are
ambassadors for Christ, as though God did beseech you by us ; we pray you in Christ's stead,
be ye reconciled to God.   For he hath made
him to be sin for us, who knew no sin ; that we
might be made the righteousness of God in Him."
In Him ; mark that.   Till we are " in Him " God
has not met us ; but when we unite ourselves
to Him by simple trust, then we, too, are " in
Him," and the Father embraces us, and falls upon our necks and kisses us.

But now, having made these needful qualifica-
tions, let us seek to discover what is involved in
the reception here described, the orders given to
the servants, and the banquet subsequent thereto.

The reception indicates loving and complete
restoration to the position which has been for-
feited by sin.   The father uttered no taunting
word ; but his whole procedure showed that he
took back his son into his affection and into his
place in the family.   Now, similarly, God " upbraideth not."   When, among men, one goes
against a father's or a friend's advice, and brings
upon himself the evils which had been described
as sure to follow his projected course, the temptation is very strong—usually, indeed, too strong to

be resisted—to say, "I told you so. You have deserved all that has come upon you. You have nobody to blame but yourself." But nothing of this sort comes from God to the repenting sinner. The past is past. God forgets as well as forgives. We might, indeed, almost be afraid to use such a term regarding Him, but He has used it himself. He says, "I will not remember thy sins;" nay, as if to impress vividly on our minds that nothing of upbraiding will ever come from Him to us, the prophet says (Micah vii. 19), "Thou wilt cast all their sins into the depths of the sea;" and Hezekiah, realizing this truth from the human side, says to Jehovah (Isaiah xxxviii. 17), "Thou hast cast all my sins behind thy back." Wondrous truth this, that when God receives us, He makes no reference to the past, nor in any way whatever painfully reminds us of our ingratitude and disobedience. Truly, when we think of it, we may say with David, in the first joy of his own fresh forgiveness, "Blessed is he whose transgression is forgiven, whose sin is covered. Blessed is the man unto whom the Lord imputeth not iniquity, and in whose spirit there is no guile."

But though God does not upbraid the returning sinner with his guilt, we must not suppose that the penitent himself does not feel it keenly. Nay, rather, the loving-kindness of his Father only makes him all the more sensible of the heinousness of his iniquity. Observe, it was after the embrace of the father, not before it, that the prodigal sobbed out his confession. He did not say within himself, " It is all right. He has taken me back without a word, and there is now no need for me to say a syllable about my folly ; so I will not use the words which I had resolved to employ." No; for this new and unexpected love made him feel more intensely than ever what a fool he had been, and how miserably he had misunderstood his father. Hence, though he had been sincere when first he thought of making a confession, he makes it now with a depth and a fervor to which his heart had been heretofore a stranger. Now, it is quite similar with the penitent. At no time does he feel the heinousness of his sin so much, as when he is rejoicing in God's forgiving love. This is indeed the glory of the gospel, that, though it proclaims pardon, it does so in such a way that, in the very act of believing the proclamation and accepting the forgiveness, the sinner sees and hates his iniquity as he never did before. Nor need this astonish us ; for the gospel shows us more thoroughly the heart of that Father whom we have slighted ; and while faith in it may keep us, yea, must keep us, from desiring to be like " one of his hired servants," it will also lead us all the more earnestly to sob out the confession, " Father, I have sinned against heaven, and in thy sight, and am no more worthy to be called thy son."

The orders given to the servants, " to put the best robe " on the prodigal, and " to put a ring on his hand, and shoes on his feet," were designed to give to the returned one the means of occupying the position and performing the duties to which he had been restored. The gift of the robe reminds us of the words of Zechariah regarding the vision of Joshua, in the third chapter of his prophecies : "*Now Joshua was clothed with filthy garments, and stood before the angel. And he answered and spake unto those that stood before him, saying, Take away the filthy garments from him. And unto him he said, Behold, I have caused thine iniquity to pass from thee, and I will clothe thee with change of raiment. And I said, Let them set a fair mitre upon his head. So they set a fair mitre upon his head, and clothed him with garments. And the angel of the Lord stood* *by*."* The ring, again, recalls to our remembrance the honor done to Joseph by Pharaoh, when the king "*took off his ring from his hand and put it upon Joseph's hand, and arrayed him in vestments of fine linen, and put a chain of gold about his neck ;*"† while the shoes were designed to be a badge of sonship, for the slave was not permitted to have sandalled feet. Everything here is thus in keeping with the customs of Oriental life ; but in giving a spiritual interpretation, it is difficult to say whether we should be content with regarding the particulars in the aggregate as a description of the fullness of the restoration to sonship, to which I have already adverted, or whether we should take each separately, as denoting some individual blessing of the gospel. No doubt the former is the correct principle of expression ; yet, it requires an effort to resist the temptation to see in the " best robe " the emblem of the Redeemer's righteousness, clothed in which the believer becomes " comely with His comeliness put upon him ; " in " the ring, " the token of assurance, or, perhaps, of that " sealing of the Spirit until the day of

---

* Zechariah, iii. 3–5. † Genesis xli. 42.

redemption," of which Paul speaks ; and in the
" shoes," that " preparation " or readiness " of
the gospel of peace," which is mentioned by the
apostle in his enumeration of the various pieces
of the Christian armor, and by which the child
of God is fitted for " walking up and down in
His name," and, "running in the way of His
commandments." But without unduly pressing
these analogies, it is more satisfactory to rest in
the general truth intended to be illustrated, which
undoubtedly is, that though his former portion had been sinfully squandered, the prodigal
was restored, not only to his father's love, but
also to his place in the family; and this just
means that the believing sinner is taken back
into God's favor, and replaced in the position
which he would have occupied if he had never
fallen.

But what is the spiritual meaning of the feast?
Some look upon the fatted calf as the emblem
of the sacrifice of Christ ; others view it as
symbolizing the Lord's Supper. But Trench, I
think, has given the true interpretation of the
banquet, when he takes it to allude to " the fes-
tal joy and rejoicing which is in heaven at the
sinner's return, and no less in the Church on

earth, and in his own heart also;" while Arnot puts it perhaps more simply, if also more antithetically, thus : " The feast indicates the joy of a forgiving God over a forgiven man, and the joy of a forgiven man in a forgiving God." * Thus we have here again a point of union between this parable and the two preceding. The one great purpose of them all was, to illustrate the fact that " there is joy in heaven over one sinner that repenteth ;" but the peculiarity here is not that the joy is greater over the recovery of that which had been lost, than over those who had never gone astray, nor that the gladness is participated in by unfallen beings, but rather in this, that *the delight is shared by the recovered one himself ;* and, in accordance with the plan which we have pursued of restricting ourselves to that which is distinctive in each of these stories, we shall confine our attention to this alone. The feast was made in honor of the prodigal. It was given specially and peculiarly to him. Others, of course, partook of it, and, more particularly, his father enjoyed the festival ; but what most of

---

* "The Parables of our Lord," by the Rev. Willian Arnot, p. 440.

all comes out here is, that the lost son had a joyous feast given to him on his welcome home.
The joy of God and of the angels has been already considered. Here we have the gladness of
the converted soul itself ; and if we keep this
prominently before our minds, we shall not fall
into the common mistake of supposing that the
scene of this banquet is confined to heaven.
Doubtless, so far as God and the angels are
concerned, we must so regard it ; but in respect
to the lost but now restored son, we must think
of it as on earth and in his own soul. The
new life begins in feast. The child of God has
" joy " as well as " peace in believing." While
God rejoices over him, he rejoices in God ; and
in the hour of conversion this gladness is peculiarly intense ; so much so, indeed, that it may
well be described as a special era of high festival. When Philip preached in the Samaritan
city, and multitudes were turned unto the Lord
under his ministrations, we read that " there was
great joy in that city ;" and when the Ethiopian
eunuch had found the salvation that is in Christ
Jesus, we are told that " he went on his way
rejoicing." So it ever is. The moment in which
salvation is embraced is one of gladness, and

the Christian life may be described as a perpetual feast. Not always, indeed, is this joy present in the same degree, nor do all possess it in the same measure, for differences of temperament and constitution manifest themselves in this as in other things ; but it is always to some extent the portion of the believer on earth, and in heaven it shall be pure and perfect and perennial. Many illustrative cases might be gleaned from Christian biography in proof of the existence and intensity of this spiritual joy in the convert's heart; but we cannot now enter upon so wide a field. Suffice it to say, that the holiest, most elevating, and most lasting gladness which the soul can feel, is that which springs from the contemplation of God's mercy, revealed to it and received by it through the cross of Christ. Peter used not the words of wild fanaticism, but the language of sober truth, when he said, " *In whom, though now we see him not, yet believing, we rejoice with joy unspeakable, and full of glory ;* and some among us can indorse the words of Mrs. Isabella Graham, when, referring to her own conversion, she says : " *My views then were dark compared with what they are now ; but this I remember, that, at the time, I felt* *heart-satisfying trust in the mercy of God through Christ, and for a time rejoiced with joy scarcely supportable, singing almost continually the hundred and third Psalm.*"* Such, my brethren, is the banquet which God spreads for the returning sinner; •but we may not forget that He makes both the Church on earth and the Church in heaven sharers with Him in His joy. They all alike make merry—I like the homely word— over a sinner's conversion; and though, on the principle that it is more blessed to give than to receive, the highest delight is that of God, yet we must not forget the gladness of the penitent himself. Sinner, do you want to be happy? Then return to God. Away from Him you must ever be in want, hungering after the world's husks, which yet cannot be obtained; but from Him you will receive the truest joy —the joy of forgiveness, the joy of acceptance, the joy of assurance, the joy of holiness, and, finally, as the climax and consummation of them all, the joy of heaven. They speak falsely who allege that the gospel is a melan-

---

* Life of Mrs. Isabella Graham, published by the American Tract Society, p. 150.

choly thing, and an enemy to mirth. " True piety is cheerful as the day," and the Christian life should be continous joy.

In the old dispensation there were three great annual festivals at which the sons of Abraham went up to Jerusalem—that of the passover, which commemorated and renewed their gladness over their deliverance from the Egyptian house of bondage.; that of the first fruits when the earliest ripe sheaves gave joyous foretoken of the coming harvest; and that of Tabernacles, when, for a season their tent-life was renewed, and they blessed God for their settled enjoyment of the promised land. But what was temporary and occasional in the former economy, is permanent under the gospel, and the gladness of all these three festivals is united in the Christian life. The Pascal joy of deliverance—the Pentecostal gladness of first fruits in the possession of the earnest of the Spirit—and the Tabernacle-rejoicing in the contemplation from out the frail booth of the flesh of " the city which hath foundations whose builder and maker is God "—these all combine to make the experience of the believer a continuous feast, which is not the less real because it is internal and spir-

itual. Three feasts in one ! and the festival-time
a life-time ! Is there nothing in all this to al-
lure us ? " Christ our passover is sacrificed for
us, therefore let us keep the feast " our life-time
through, " not with the old leaven of malice and
wickedness, but with the unleavened bread of sin-
cerity and truth." *

---

* 1 Corinthians, v., 7, 8.

THE PRODIGAL SON.

IV.

THE ELDER BROTHER.

"Now his elder son was in the field ; and as he came and drew nigh to the house, he heard music and dancing.

"And he called one of the servants, and asked what these things meant.

"And he said unto him, Thy brother is come ; and thy father hath killed the fatted calf, because he hath received him safe and sound.

"And he was angry, and would not go in ; therefore came his father out, and entreated him.

"And he, answering, said to his father, Lo, these many years do I serve thee ; neither transgressed I at any time thy commandment ; and yet thou never gavest me a kid, that I might make merry with my friends :

"But as soon as this thy son was come, which hath devoured thy living with harlots, thou hast killed for him the fatted calf.

"And he said unto him, Son, thou art ever with me, and all that I have is thine.

"It was meet that we should make merry, and be glad ; for this thy brother was dead, and is alive again ; and was lost, and is found."

LUKE xv., 25-32.

THE PRODIGAL SON.

IV.

THE ELDER BROTHER.

In the general household joy over the prodigal's return, there was one who refused to share. The elder son, who now for the first time comes into prominence, and who seems to have had very large ideas of his own importance, was absent in the field at the moment of his brother's re-appearance, and only became aware that something unwonted had occurred when, as he drew near, he heard the sound of music and dancing. Instead, however, of going trustfully forward into the house, in the full confidence that everything over which his father presided must be right and proper, he showed his mean and suspicious disposition by

calling one of the servants, and asking of him what
"these things meant." Promptly and plainly,
the domestic made reply, "Thy brother is come;
and thy father hath killed for him the fatted calf,
because he hath received him safe and sound."
The servant's words imply that, in his view, it
was the most natural thing in the world that such
a festival should be held on such an occasion;
but the information which he conveyed was
gall and wormwood to the elder brother's soul.
"What! such a fuss made over the return of a
useless good-for-nothing! Never was any like
rejoicing made on my account. Is this, then, the
reward of all my steadiness and industry? Let
them keep feast who please, but I will take no
place at the board." And so, in the sulks, because
more seemed to be made of his brother than of
himself, he refused to enter the house. But his
father could not think of allowing him to remain
in this mood, without at least making an effort
to induce him to change his purpose. The same
love that prompted him, when he saw his younger
son returning, to go forth to meet him, disposed
him now, when he saw his elder son departing, to
go out and entreat him to come in. But he was
met in an unfilial and almost insulting man-

ner. " Lo, these many years do I *serve* thee "—
(what! a son, and yet talking of service in this
mercantile fashion !—where has thy filial affection
gone? Has it been for the reward, then, after all,
and not for love, that thou hast staid at home ?)
—"neither transgressed I at any time thy commandment "—(excellent young man! truly thou
hast a good report of thyself. A very model son !
A perfect specimen of obedience to the Fifth
Commandment ! and yet, methinks, had thy sonship been as faultless as thou sayest, it would have
been also somewhat unconscious of its merit. I
like not this dwelling on thy pre-eminence. There
is more true sonship in thy brother's, " I have
sinned," than in thy self-laudation)—" and yet
thou never gavest me a kid that I might make
merry with my friends "—(Didst thou ever ask it?
or was there ever any great occasion in thy life
when such a thing would have been appropriate ?
Besides, the fatted calf was killed, not to give a
banquet to thy brother's friends, but to express
thy father's own delight. Why wilt thou think
thyself slighted, when no offence was intended
toward thee ?)—" But as soon as this thy son was
come "—(Thy son ! Is he not then thy brother
also? or dost thou repudiate the relationship ?

What an insult to thy father is this sneering phrase!)—"who hath devoured thy living with harlots"—(Ah! how envy exaggerates the faults of those whose good it grudges, and imputes to them wickednesses of its own imagining! The prodigal had not devoured all the father's living; there was a good fat portion yet for the elder son; and as to his wasting his substance on harlots, that is an unsupported assertion on the part of his brother. It may have been true. But there is no evidence that it was. Envy, however, takes it quite for granted. Your very precise and proper people, who pride themselves most upon never having transgressed any commandment, have always most to say about other people's faults, and they take good care to make them blacker by their speech.)

We have thus parenthetically exposed the ungenerous insinuations and unfilial disposition of this youth's complaint, in order that we may bring out before you more clearly the magnanimity of his father, who takes no notice of the sneering innuendoes which were designed to be so stinging, but only calmly replies, "Son, thou art ever with me, and all that I have is thine." As if he had said, "Why speak of

making merry with thy friends, when thou hast
always had a feast in me; and as for thy brother's waste, say no more of that; thou art not
the poorer on that account, for all that I have
is thine." But this is all the length the father will go; he will not acknowledge that he
had in any way overlooked the one son, in his
joy over the return of the other; nor will he
admit that he had done anything strange or im-
proper in making such a festival. On the contrary, he defends his procedure, and repeats his
gladness, at one and the same time, saying, "It
was meet," *i.e.*, it was fitting;—it was in every
respect in harmony with the dictates of nature
and religion—it was in the highest degree
appropriate,—"that we should make merry and
be glad; for this thy brother was dead, and
is alive again; and was lost, and is found."
Observe the delicate reproof conveyed in the
first word, "son," and in that other expression, "thy brother." On the former occasion
he said, "This my son was dead, and is
alive again; but now it is "thy brother." It
was as if he had said, "I have observed the
spirit of a servant in all that thou hast said,
but I will still call thee 'son;' and though thou

cynically didst refuse to call the returned wanderer ' thy brother,' I will not let thee act so
utterly unworthily. Thou wilt think better of it
yet. Somewhere in thee, surely, there is a brother's heart; and if that be touched, thou wilt
at once admit the ' meetness' of our mirth."

Thus far I have had regard only to the literal
aspect of the story, and I cannot pass from that,
without pausing a moment or two longer to
point out two things which come out here, which
may be wholesome to us all.

Observe how self-importance makes a man
moody and unhappy. He who is always thinking of his own excellences, renders himself thereby unfit to enjoy the good of others, and is prone
to imagine that every token of affection given to
another is an insult offered to himself. Hence he
is touchy, sensitive, irritable and envious. He
takes offence where none is meant, and even
when those around him are not thinking of
him at all, he interprets their conduct as if it
were studiously discourteous, and goes through
the world smarting from wounds which have
sprung, not so much from the neglect of others, as
from his own overweening self-conceit. There
is no surer way to make ourselves miserable

than to think of ourselves more highly than we ought to think. It isolates us from all about us. It cuts us off alike from human sympathy and divine assistance. It makes us very Ishmaels, with our hands against every man, and every man's hands apparently against us. It gives a jaundiced interpretation to the behavior of those who, so far from meaning to do evil to us, have our best interests at heart, and love us with self-sacrificing affection. The man who has a wound about him, no matter where it may be, feels it to be always in his way. Let him do what he will, or go where he may, he cannot move himself but he is conscious of its pain. In like manner, he who has this feeling of self-importance is continually smarting. Somebody has always been slighting him. He is constantly complaining of having been insulted, and when honor is given to another, he feels nothing but that *he* has been overlooked. Thus he shuts himself out from every festival, and mopes most of all when others are merry. May God deliver us from this idolatry of self, on whose altar all true nobleness and real happiness are completely immolated!

Notice, again, how repulsive to others this self

important spirit is. You cannot take to this elder brother. Even in his wanderings and sins, the younger was more lovable than he, his industry and sobriety notwithstanding. So it is ever with the selfish one. He is a non-conductor in society. The electricity of love never passes through him; and in the end, all loving hearts are driven from him. Thus he is not only the most unhappy, but also the most useless of men. The "*selfist*" is left, in righteous retribution, to that most miserable of all companions, himself. He has no magnetism about him. He can gain no entrance into the hearts of others. He stands on the outside of every holy enterprise, and is at the very antipodes of him who said, "Neither count I my life dear unto myself, that I may finish my course with joy, and the ministry that I have received of the Lord." Thus, alike to do good and to be happy, we must forget *self ;* we must merge ourselves in the cause which we are seeking to advance; we must be, as one has phrased it, "emptied and lost and swallowed up in Christ."

But passing now to the interpretation of the parable, the question arises, "Who is this elder brother?" Various answers have been given.

Some have said that he represents the angels in their relation to the human race, but this can scarcely be maintained; for, as the other two parables in this chapter make evident, so far from being envious at the reception given by God to returning sinners of mankind, the angels rejoice with Him. This view, therefore, must be conclusively set aside. Others have found those represented by the elder brother in the Jews, while the younger is taken by them to symbolize the Gentiles; and it must be confessed that much may be advanced in favor of this explanation. As a nation the Jews were most exclusive, and the very idea of the Gentiles being made partakers with them of the blessings of the covenant was most repugnant to them. Thus when our Lord, in his first sermon at Nazareth, referred to Elijah's mission to Sarepta, and Elisha's cure of Naaman, and thereby suggested that the Gentiles were to be made sharers of the favors which had been so long restricted to the Jews, His hearers were so enraged that they laid violent hands upon Him, and sought to slay Him. So, again, when Paul addressed the crowd from the castle stairs at Jerusalem, they gave him a patient hearing until

he spoke of the Gentiles; but immediately there-
after they cried, "Away with such a fellow
from the earth; it is not fit that he should live."
Nay, so strong was this feeling even in the breast
of Peter, the apostle, that he had to be prepared
by a special vision from heaven for preaching
the gospel to the Gentile Cornelius. There is no
doubt, therefore, that the spirit of the elder brother here was manifested by the Jews in their
treatment of the Gentiles. But whether this
was the primary reference of the appendix to
the parable of the prodigal, is another matter. The occasion on which it was spoken is
described in the opening verses of the chapter;
and though we have there an allusion to the
Scribes and Pharisees as over against the
publicans and sinners, yet I fail to see any hint
of nationality. These different classes or charac-
ters were all Jews alike; and therefore it seems
to me to be not only an unwarrantable restriction
of the scope of the parable, but also a mistaken
idea of its original application, to say that the
elder brother represents the Jew. Others, therefore, understand that the purpose of Jesus in
introducing the elder brother into this parable
was to hold up a mirror to the Scribes and Phari-

sees, in which each of them might see himself,
and might thus comprehend, not only how unamiable he was, but also how little there was in
common between him and God. But even this
interpretation is beset with difficulties; for how
could it be said that these Pharisees and Scribes
had never transgressed God's commandment?
and with what propriety could they be called
God's sons, or could it be affirmed that He was
ever with them, and that all that He had was
theirs? To these questions, Calvin, who may
taken as the exponent of this class of interpre-
ters, thus replies:—"He compares the Scribes,
who were swelled with presumption, to good and
modest men, who had always lived with de-
cency and sobriety, and had honorably sup-
ported their families; nay, even to obedient
children, who, throughout their whole lives, had
patiently submitted to their father's control. And
though they were utterly unworthy of this com-
mendation, yet Christ, speaking according to
their belief, attributes to them, by way of con-
cession, their pretended holiness as if it had
been virtue, as if He had said, Though I were
to grant to you what you falsely boast of that
you have always been obedient children to God,

still you ought not so haughtily and cruelly to reject your brethren when they repent of their wicked life."* To those who accept this explanation as satisfactory, the parable has a precise and distinct reference to the Pharisees and Scribes ; and in this view, the uncertainty in which we are left as to whether the elder brother went in to the feast or not, becomes very suggestive, as being in itself an appeal to the self-righteous ones to whom it was addressed, to reconsider their position, if haply they might, as we know some of them afterwards did, go in, and hold high festival with God's redeemed ones, brought from the very lowest of the people.

Others, however, dissatisfied with all the interpretations which I have enumerated, and pressed especially with the difficulty, that the elder brother seems to be regarded as a true, though temporarily erring son, have preferred to make him stand as the representative of those who, as Matthew Henry says, are " really good, and have been so from their youth up, and never went astray into any vicious course of living ; to whom, therefore,

---

* *Commentary in loco.*

those words, 'Son, thou art ever with me,' are ap-
plicable without any difficulty, though they are
not so to the Scribes and Pharisees."

Now, if it were necessary to adopt any one of
these explanations, to the exclusion of all the rest,
I should, without hesitation, prefer that which regards the elder brother as the likeness of the
Scribes and Pharisees, believing that, though it is
by no means free from difficulty, it is yet the most
pointed and natural interpretation of them all.
Still, I do not see that we are called to identify
this self-sufficient and unamiable youth with any
particular individual. To me he stands out rather
as the idealized representative of a disposition or
character. He is the impersonation and embodi-
ment of envy; and wherever, or in whomsoever,
that quality exists, there you have, for the time
being, the elder brother. I gladly avail myself
here of Mr. Arnot's words :—" In representing the
human figure, an artist may proceed upon either
of two distinct principles, according to the object
which for the time he may have in view. He may,
on the one hand, delineate the likeness of an individual, producing a copy of his particular features, with all their beauties and all their blem-
ishes alike; or he may, on the other hand, con-

ceive and execute an ideal picture of man, the portrait of no person in particular, with features selected from many specimens of the race, and combined in one complete figure. The parable of the prodigal is a picture of the latter kind; it is not, out and out, the picture of any man, but it is to a certain extent the picture of every man."* Thus viewed, the elder brother also is an ideal picture, not agreeing in every minute particular with any one man, or any one class of men, but yet so portraying the workings of one evil disposition that the envious man in him may see himself, whether he be a Pharisee or Scribe, standing outside of the spiritual Church of Christ altogether, or a genuine but imperfect disciple, who is really connected with the Lord Jesus. This explanation, while it gets rid of the difficulties which must meet every one who attempts to give a distinct interpretation to every expression employed by, or addressed to, the elder brother, has the further merit that it widens the application of the parable, making it speak to the genuine believer in Christ, as well as to the legalist and the self-righteous. Take the elder brother as representing the concrete

---

* The Parables of our Lord, p. 431.

Pharisee, and very few will be inclined to think that he has anything to do with them. Take him, on the other hand, as the dramatic delineation of the working of the self-righteous and envious spirit, and each of us must feel that there is a great deal of *elder-brotherliness* about himself. In the legalist there is nothing else but this evil disposition; but there is more or less of it even in the true follower of Christ; and so the elder brother stands out here as a warning to all, and none of us can say with truth that he has no message to us. "Who is this elder son?" The question was once asked in an assembly of ministers at Elberfeldt. Daniel Krummacher made answer—"I know him very well; I met him only yesterday." "Who is he?" they asked, eagerly, and he replied solemnly, "Myself!" He then explained that, on the previous day, hearing that a very ill-conditioned person had received a very gracious visitation of God's goodness, he had felt not a little envy and irritation.* This was the true reading of the story, and it is capable of almost indefinite expansion and manifold application. It fits the haughty Scribes and Pharisees, to whom it was

---

* Stiers' "Words of Jesus," vol. iv., p. 162 ; quoted in Dr. James Hamilton's "Pearl of Parables," p. 164.

first addressed, and who murmured at the attention paid by Christ to publicans and sinners, saying, " This man receiveth sinners, and eateth with them." It fits the Jews in the Saviour's day, and even in the early Christian Church, who looked askance at the Gentiles, and complained that the gospel was preached to them also. It fits the disciples at Jerusalem, who, immediately after Paul's conversion, were " all afraid of him, and believed not that he was a disciple ;" and it fits Paul himself, when, in a mood of stern and somewhat unfeeling severity, he refused to take back Mark into his confidence, and had so sharp a contention with Barnabas over the affair that they departed asunder the one from the other. Truly, even of that great apostle, at that time, it might have been said, " He was angry, and would not go in." So, again, when a Christian of long-standing and irreproachable character, who has known some degree of happiness in Christ, but has not had anything approaching to ecstasy, is inclined to be suspicious of the genuineness of the transport of him who has just been converted from a life of grossest sin, and is disposed, in envy, to ask, " Why should such experiences be granted to him, while I, who have been seeking to follow

Jesus all my days, know nothing of them ?" we have the working of the same disposition as that which the elder brother here displayed. When a minister of age and excellence, who is mourning over the apparent fruitlessness of his labors, is tempted to ask how it comes that a young brother, in the very outset of his career, is made instrumental in bringing multitudes to Christ, and permits himself to think, if not to say, that it is ungenerous in God to pass by an old and faithful servant such as he has been, and to use and bless an inexperienced lad ; or when a stickler for order and decorum murmurs that the Lord should honor with success the irregularities of a revival meeting, and the labors of some " converted prize-fighter," in larger measure than he seems to bless the stated workings of the authorized ministry in the ordinary exercises of the sanctuary ; or when some father, prominent in the Church for piety and usefulness, is led, in his haste and in his self-importance, to ask, " How comes it that the children of this one and that one—of little name among the brethren, and hardly known for their zeal and devotedness—are all converted, while my son is permitted to grow up in sin, and to become to me a source of

constant anxiety ?"—in each and all of these we
have a phasis of that unlovely disposition which,
in the elder brother, is here condemned. The
Sabbath-school teacher who throws up the work
because another seems more successful in it than
himself ; the laborer in any department of benev-
olent activity, who, because he thinks that more
is made of some one else than of himself, gives
way to personal pique, and will have no more to
do with the concern ; the over-sensitive, irritable, petted man, who is forever taking offence,
and manages somehow to exclude himself from
every society with which he has been connected,
and to estrange himself from the sympathy and co-
operation of all with whom he has come into contact ; may all look here, and in the elder brother
of this parable they will behold themselves. But
let not even these imagine that they are beyond
God's acceptance. The father came out and entreated the elder brother to go in to the feast ; and
so still God is appealing to the envious. The door
is open to them, if they will but enter ; and when
they consent to do so in the spirit of a son, and
not of a servant, then they too shall rejoice, and
the festival, instead of aggravating them into

misery, will be felt to be an appropriate expression
of their mirth.

I close with three practical reflections from
the whole subject.

1. In the first place, let professing Christians
seek to manifest to sinners generally the same
spirit that God has shown to themselves. The
gentleness of God should be repeated by us, and
with the same tenderness and affection as Jesus
dealt with the ungodly, we should deal with
those whom we desire to bring in penitence to
Him. Parents, this parable speaks to you about
the training of your children, and bids you seek
their godly upbringing, not in rigorous and un-
bending sternness, but in tender love. Sabbath-
school teachers, this parable bids you, in your
earnest efforts for your scholars' welfare, show to
them the same gentleness that the father manifested when he fell weeping on the neck of his
returning son ; and it warns you against indulging
in vituperation and reproach. Had the prodigal
met the elder brother first, he might have gone
away back to his iniquity, ay, even from his
father's very door. So a cruel, unfeeling, taunting
word may be the means of sending away from
Jesus one, who else might have come to Him in

believing penitence. Pastor, there is a message here for thee too : and thou art commanded to be in the midst of thy flock, loving, as was this father to his erring son ; and to beware lest, by hard unfeeling sternness, thou shouldst drive away those who are seeking to enter into the fold. O for more of this divine tenderness among us all ! Let us remember that the reputation of the gospel, and in some sort also the character of God himself, is at stake in our conduct ; and let us tremble with a holy fear, lest we should give occasion to His enemies to blaspheme His name, or lest we should, by our repulsiveness, scare away some poor soul from the loving Father who is so willing to receive him. Men judge of God through us. Let us see, therefore, that they have, from our deportment toward them, a right idea of His willinghood to welcome them.

2. In the second place, let anxious sinners be on their guard against judging of God's attitude toward them from that which is assumed by some who call themselves His children. They may be Pharisees, and not true sons. Or they may be really children, yet, at the moment, by reason of the imperfection still adhering to them, they may be acting an unfilial part. In any case, we must

not allow the character and conduct of any man, be he official in the Church, or whatever else, to prejudice us against God. Men may repel us, and refuse to have anything whatever to do with us ; but God will receive us graciously, and love us freely. The respectable Church members in this respectable age may stand aloof from us, and may make us feel that they would consider themselves to be degraded by any fellowship with us ; but He who sat and talked with the woman of Samaria at the well, and allowed the woman that was a sinner to wash His feet with tears and wipe them with the hairs of her head, will in nowise cast us out. The minister of the gospel may even so far forget his character and privilege as to talk to us with hard and cold severity ; yea, he may treat us with rudeness or with positive injustice, but he is only a man ; he may be even a very imperfect man ; he is not God ; and let us be thankful that God is not like him. There is a magnanimous mercy, an exalted generosity in God which we look for in vain, in the same degree at least, in any man. And whatever may be the effect upon us of the actions of our fellow-mortals, we must not allow them to set us against Jehovah. He is always on the out-look for returning sinners, and before they have time to finish their confession unto Him, He is already falling in welcome on their necks. Do not, therefore, misinterpret Him by supposing that the cold-hearted exclusiveness, which is too manifest in many who profess to be His children, is in any respect characteristic of Him. Regard Him as he presents Himself to you in His word. Read Him as He has written Himself in the mission and sacrifice of His Son; and whatever else may be suggested to you by the disposition of His professed people, rest you sure of this, that His true character has been portrayed in this parable, and that Isaiah has not misrepresented Him when he says, " Let the wicked forsake his way, and the unrighteous man his thoughts, and let him return unto the Lord, for he will have mercy upon him, and unto our God, for he will abundantly pardon."

Finally, let us learn from this whole chapter the sincere, earnest, *personal* interest which God has in the salvation of sinners. I have already indicated that in each of these parables we have set before us a part at least of the work of each of the three persons of the Godhead in the redemption of man. The Son becomes incarnate,

and offers Himself a sacrifice for sin ; the Spirit
gives the truth, and secures its entrance into the
soul ; and the Father gladly welcomes the wanderer to his home again. We may surely conclude,
therefore, that everything God does in connection
with the work of salvation, is in the sinner's
interest, and with a view to secure his recovery.
There are no obstacles to man's salvation now on
God's side. If there be obstacles yet, they lie
with the sinner. Jehovah, with all the solemnity
of an oath, has said, "As I live I have no pleasure in the death of the wicked, but that the wicked turn from his way and live ;" and even more for-
cibly than by that striking asseveration has Jesus
set the same truth before us in this matchless chapter. I answer, therefore, all difficulties which the
inquirer may feel about such topics as election,
and the special agency of the Spirit, and the
sovereignty of God, and the like, by bidding him
go and read these parables. They show that God
is in earnest in seeking to save lost souls. They
prove, therefore, that everything about him, and
done by Him, is in the interest of the sinner's
return. His electing love, the enlightening agency of His Spirit, His sovereignty, are all to be
interpreted in the light of this chapter, and are

to be understood as all designed *to help*, and not *to hinder* the sinner's restoration. They are not stumbling-blocks placed in the way of the penitent, but they are agencies at work in removing obstacles from his path. See to it, therefore, that you do not misunderstand God. Meet every speculative difficulty arising from the doctrines to which I have referred, with this chapter, which has always been regarded as one of " the crown jewels " of the Christian Church. Silence every foreboding about the reception which God may give you—with these, " the first three," of the Redeemer's parables. Arise, and go in fullest confidence to thy Father. He will not reject thee, but will enfold thee in His forgiving embrace, and will say over thee, in infinite tenderness and with Divine delight—" THIS MY SON WAS DEAD, AND IS ALIVE AGAIN ; HE WAS LOST, AND IS FOUND."

THE END.

DR. HODGE'S THEOLOGY.

─o─

Systematic Theology.

BY CHARLES HODGE, D.D., LL.D.,

OF PRINCETON THEOLOGICAL SEMINARY.

─────────

Three vols. 8vo, tinted paper. Price, vols. I. and II., $4.50. *Vol. III.,* $5.

─────────

In these volumes are comprised the results of the life-long labors and investigations of one of the most eminent theologians of the age. The work covers the ground usually occupied by treatises on Systematic Theology, and adopts the commonly received divisions of the subject,—THEOLOGY, Vol. I.; ANTHROPOLOGY, Vol. II.; SOTERIOLOGY AND ESCHATOLOGY, Vol. III.

The plan of the author is to state and vindicate the teachings of the Bible on these various subjects, and to examine the antagonistic doctrines of different classes of Theologians. His book, therefore, is intended to be both didactic and elenchtic.

The various topics are discussed with that close and keen analytical and logical power, combined with that simplicity, lucidity, and strength of style which have already given DR. HODGE a world-wide reputation as a controversialist and writer, and as an investigator of the great theological problems of the day.

─────o─────

SPECIAL NOTICE.

Volumes I. and II. of DR. HODGE'S *SYSTEMATIC THEOLOGY are now published. Vol. III. will be ready early in November.*

₊ *A supplementary volume, containing an analysis of the whole work, prepared by* Prof. A. A. HODGE, *of Alleghany Seminary, an index of topics and also one of Scriptural texts, is in course of preparation, and will be issued early in* 1873.

SCRIBNER, ARMSTRONG & CO.,

654 BROADWAY, NEW YORK.

The Minister's Library.

TWENTY VOLUMES
AND FIFTY DOLLARS' WORTH OF BOOKS FOR
THIRTY DOLLARS.

A Rare Chance for Ministers and Students!

In order to bring within the reach of Clergymen and Students of the most moderate means some of their leading standard works, Messrs. Scribner, Armstrong & Co. announce the issue of

THE MINISTER'S LIBRARY.

As will be seen from the list below, this Library includes a number of the most valuable works ever published in this country, in the various departments of Religion, Literature, Exegesis, Homiletics, Sacred History, description of the Holy Land, the Life of Christ and of St. Paul. with a choice selection of Sermons by some of the most famous American divines, are all included in the Library ; and, by a special arrangement, the series is placed at so low a price that every student and minister can afford to purchase it. The volumes, if bought singly, would cost FIFTY DOLLARS, while the set is furnished at THIRTY DOLLARS. THE MINISTER'S LIBRARY includes :

No. of Vols.

ALEXANDER'S (Dr. J. W.)....Consolation			1
ALEXANDER'S (Dr. J. A.) ....Isaiah			2
do.	do.	.....Psalms	2
do.	do.	.....Sermons	1
ADAMS (Dr. Wm.)............Thanksgiving			1
ANDREWS (Rev. S. J.)........Life of Our Lord			1
BUSHNELL'S..................Nature and the Supernatural.........			1
CONYBEARE & HOWSON'S..St. Paul			2
FISHER'S (Prof. Geo. P.)......Supernatural Origin of Christianity..			1
HURST'S (Prof. J. F.)..........History of Rationalism			1
LILLIE'S (Dr. John)............Lectures on Peter			1
SHEDD (Dr. W. G. T.)........Sermons to the Natural Man			1
STANLEY'S (Dean)............History of the Jewish Church			2
do. do. ....History of the Eastern Church			1
THOMPSON'S (Dr. J. P.)......Theology of Christ			1
WOOLSEY (Dr. T. D.)...... ...Religion of the Present and Future..			1

SPECIAL NOTICE.

THE MINISTER'S LIBRARY will be sold only in sets. The volumes comprised in it may be had in the styles in which they were formerly issued, at the old prices ; but under no circumstances will the works, as printed for this Library, be sold separately.

THE MINISTER'S LIBRARY *may be had of all booksellers, or it will be sent, express charges paid, by the publishers on receipt of the price,* $30.

SCRIBNER, ARMSTRONG & CO.,
654 BROADWAY, NEW YORK.

Prices and Styles of the Different Editions

OF

FROUDE'S HISTORY OF ENGLAND.

The Chelsea Edition.

In half roan, gilt top, per set of twelve vols. 12mo... ....$21.00

Elegance and cheapness are combined in a remarkable degree in this edition. It takes its name from the place of Mr. Froude's residence in London, also famous as the home of Thomas Carlyle.

The Popular Edition.

In cloth, at the rate of $1.25 per volume. The set (12 vols.), in a neat box.$15.00
The Same, in half calf extra... 30.00

This edition is printed from the same plates as the other editions, and on firm, white paper. It is, without exception, the cheapest set of books of its class ever issued in this country.

The Library Edition.

In twelve vols. crown 8vo, cloth.......... ... .$30.00
The Same, in half calf extra... 50.00

The Edition is printed on laid and tinted paper, at the Riverside Press, and is in every respect worthy a place in the most carefully selected library.

SHORT STUDIES ON GREAT SUBJECTS.

BY JAMES ANTHONY FROUDE, M.A.,
"*History of England,*" "*The English in Ireland during the Eighteenth Century,*" etc.

POPULAR EDITION. Two vols. 12mo, cloth, $1.50 per vol. The Set....$3.00
CHELSEA EDITION. Two vols. 12mo, half roan, gilt top, $2.00 per volume. Per Set.. .... 4.00

The Complete Works of James Anthony Froude, M.A.

HISTORY OF ENGLAND AND SHORT STUDIES.
Fourteen vols., in a neat Box.

POPULAR EDITION..$18.00
CHELSEA EDITION... 25.00

The above works sent, post-paid, by the publishers, on receipt of the price

SCRIBNER, ARMSTRONG & CO.,

654 BROADWAY, NEW YORK.

LANGE'S COMMENTARY.

NOW READY:

ANOTHER OLD TESTAMENT VOLUME.

The Psalms.

Translated and Edited by Rev. Drs. CONANT *and* FORSYTH, *and* Revs. C. A. BRIGGS *and* G. McCURDY.

One vol. royal 8vo, 800 pages, cloth.... ....$5.00

The Volumes previously Published are:

OLD TESTAMENT.—I. GENESIS. II. JOSHUA, JUDGES, AND RUTH. III. FIRST AND SECOND KINGS. IV. PROVERBS, SONG OF SOLOMON, ECCLESIASTES. V. JEREMIAH AND LAMENTATION.

NEW TESTAMENT.—I. MATTHEW. II. MARK AND LUKE. III. JOHN. IV. ACTS. V. THE EPISTLE OF PAUL TO THE ROMANS. VI. CORINTHIANS. VII. GALATIANS, EPHESIANS PHILIPPIANS, COLOSSIANS. VIII. THESSALONIANS, TIMO-THY, TITUS, PHILEMON, AND HEBREWS. IX. THE EPIS-TLES GENERAL OF JAMES, PETER, JOHN AND JUDE.

Each one vol. 8vo. Price per vol., in half calf, $7.50; in sheep, $6.50; in cloth, $5.00.

NAMES AND DENOMINATIONS OF CONTRIBUTORS.

W. G. T. SHEDD, D.D., Presbyterian.
E. A. WASHBURNE, D.D., Episcopal.
A. C. KENDRICK, D.D., Baptist.
W. H. GREEN, D.D., Presbyterian.
J. F. HURST, D.D., Methodist.
TAYLER LEWIS, LL.D., Dutch Reformed.
Rev. CH. F. SHAFFER, D.D., Lutheran.
R. D. HITCHCOCK, D.D., Presbyterian.
E. HARWOOD, D.D., Episcopal.
H. B. HACKETT, D.D., Baptist.
JOHN LILLIE, D.D., Presbyterian.
Rev. W. G. SUMNER, Episcopal.
Prof. CHARLES ELLIOTT, Presbyterian.
THOS. C. CONANT, D.D., Baptist.

E. D. YEOMANS, D.D., Presbyterian.
Rev. C. C. STARBUCK, Congregational.
J. ISIDOR MOMBERT, D.D., Episcopal.
D. W. POOR, D.D., Presbyterian
C. P. WING, D.D., Presbyterian.
GEORGE E. DAY, D.D., Congregational.
Rev. P. H. STEENSTRA, Episcopal.
A. GOSMAN, D.D., Presbyterian.
Pres. CHAS. A. AIKEN, D.D., Presbyt'n.
M. B. RIDDLE, D.D., Dutch Reformed.
Prof. WM. WELLS, D.D., Methodist.
W. H. HORNBLOWER, D.D., Presbyt'n.
Prof. GEORGE BLISS, Baptist.
T. W. CHAMBERS, D.D., Reformed.

☞ Each volume of "LANGE'S COMMENTARY" is complete in itself, and can be purchased separately. Sent, post-paid, to any address upon receipt of the price ($5 per volume) by the publishers,

SCRIBNER, ARMSTRONG & CO.,
654 BROADWAY, NEW YORK.

www.ingramcontent.com/pod-product-compliance
Lightning Source LLC
Chambersburg PA
CBHW020001030726
47500CB00002B/389